JULIETA AND

THE
DIAMOND
ENIGMA

JULIETA AND THE DIAMOND ENIGMA

LUISANA DUARTE ARMENDÁRIZ

TU BOOKS

AN IMPRINT OF LEE & LOW BOOKS INC.

NEW YORK

TU BOOKS, an imprint of LEE & LOW BOOKS Inc.
95 Madison Avenue, New York, NY 10016
leeandlow.com

Manufactured in the United States of America

Printed on paper from responsible sources

Book design by Sammy Yuen
Edited by Elise McMullen-Ciotti
Interior illustrations by Sammy Yuen and McKenzie Mayle
Cover art by Olivia Aserr
Book production by The Kids at Our House
The text is set in Cochin

10 9 8 7 6 5 4 3 2 1
First Edition

Library of Congress Cataloging-in-Publication Data
Names: Duarte Armendáriz, Luisana, author.
Title: Julieta and the diamond enigma / Luisana Duarte Armendáriz.
Description: First edition. | New York : Tu Books, an imprint of Lee & Low Books Inc.,
    [2020] | Audience: Ages 8-12. | Audience: Grades 4-6. |
Summary: When a diamond goes missing from the Louvre, it is up to nine-year-old Julieta
    to identify the thief, exonerate her father, and return home to Boston before her baby
    brother is born. Includes glossary of French and Spanish words and notes about the
    Regent Diamond, Athena, and works of art mentioned in the book.
Identifiers: LCCN 2020001613 (print) | LCCN 2020001614 (ebook) | ISBN 9781643790466
    (hardcover) | ISBN 9781643790473 (epub) | ISBN 9781643790480 (mobi)
Subjects: CYAC: Art museums—Fiction. | Stealing—Fiction. | Hispanic Americans—
    Fiction. | Boston (Mass.)—Fiction. | Paris (France)—Fiction. | France—Fiction. |
    Mystery and detective stories.
Classification: LCC PZ7.1.D825 Ju 2020 (print) | LCC PZ7.1.D825 (ebook) |
    DDC [Fic]—dc23
LC record available at https://lccn.loc.gov/2020001613
LC ebook record available at https://lccn.loc.gov/2020001614

*To my parents, who gave me everything
and so much more.*

To Chelis, my buddy in the trenches.

Note for Readers

Julieta is bilingual and speaks both English and Spanish. In this story, she also learns a little French while having her adventure in Paris, France. If you'd like to learn what some of the words mean, you can refer back to these pages and look them up. You can also learn more about the art pieces Julieta sees in the museums beginning on page 203.

Glossary of French and Spanish Words

FRENCH WORDS

arrêt (ah-**ret**): stop
bonjour (bon-zhoor): good morning, good day
dans la galerie (dahn la gal-air-ee): inside the hall
Il est interdit d'entrer la fontaine! (Eel ay ahn-tur-dee dahn-tray la fon-**tan**): It's prohibited to enter the fountain!
Je comprends. (zhuh com-**prahn**): I understand.
ma chèrie (mah **share**-ee): my dear

mademoiselle (mad-mwah-zel): miss

merci (mare-see): thank you

mon dieu (mon dyuh): my god

monsieur (miss-syur): sir

oui (wee): yes

s'il vous plait (seel voo play): please

sortie (sore-tee): exit

touché (too-**shay**): nicely said or done

très jolie (tray zho-lee): very pretty

SPANISH WORDS

amor (ah-**more**): love, used as an endearing expression, like "honey" or "sweetie"

corazón (co-rah-**sone**): heart, used as an endearing expression, like "honey" or "sweetie"

empalagada (ehm-pahl-ah-gahd-ah): Being in a state of having eaten something too sweet or rich. Also used to describe the use of extreme sentiment.

dios mío (dee-ohs **mee**-oh): my god

Estoy muy cansada. (es-**toy** moo-ee can-**sahd**-ah): I am very tired.

gracias (grah-see-ahs): thank you

hogar, dulce hogar (oh-**gahr, dool**-seh oh-**gahr**): home, sweet home

hola (oh-lah): hello

m'ija (mee-hah): contraction of "my daughter," used as an endearing expression, like "honey" or "sweetie"

Mucho ayuda el que no estorba. (moo-cho ah-**you**-dah ehl keh no es-**tor**-bah): The one that doesn't bother you, helps a lot.

No me gustan los caracoles. (noh meh **goo**-stan los kah-rah-**co**-less): I don't like snails.

sí (see): yes

Soy tu hermana. (Soy too ehr-**man**-ah): I'm your sister.

Te extraño. (teh ex-**trah**-nyo): I miss you.

THERE ARE ONLY TWO PURPLE PINS ON THE WORLD map. They tease me all the way from across Mom and Dad's study.

The multicolored pins mark the countries each of the members of my family have visited. Only two purple pins in a sea of blue and red. That will change very soon. Tomorrow I'll call Mom from France and kindly ask her to add another one to the map. I'm trying hard not to be, as Dad calls it, *petty* about the situation. He says I'll have more than enough time to travel all over the world when I'm older. I say if I ever want to fill the whole map with my pins, I should already have at least five on there now that I'm nine. Otherwise, I'll never make it to all one hundred and ninety-six countries. Still, three pins are better than two.

One of the purple pins currently on the wall is placed on the United States, home sweet home. The other is proudly pinned on México, the result of visiting my family during a whole month last summer. I remember my grandparents and cousins. I remember the cities we visited. The colors and the music. And how I didn't have to explain that the *J* in Julieta sounds like the hooting of an owl. Like *whoooo*-lieta. But what I remember the most is eating elotes with cheese, butter, and chile every night for the first week and a half. I shouldn't have overdone it. I got sick afterward. I couldn't play with my cousins anymore, and I actually wasn't allowed to eat anything other than caldo de pollo con verduras for about three days. Breakfast, lunch, and dinner — only chicken soup.

Maybe that's what King Midas and I have in common. I'm currently reading about him in one of my favorite books. He and I both want more of the things we love. Me, elotes. Him, gold. Oh, boy, did King Midas love his gold. He loved and wanted so much of it that when he was granted a magical wish, he wished for the power to touch any object and turn it into gold. That kind of backfired on him, since he ended up being unable to eat, drink, or even hug his family. Reading this story has made me promise myself that when I visit México again, I won't eat elotes every night . . . at least, no more than two nights in a row.

I look up at the map again and stare at those purple pins.

"Soon," I tell them.

2

BLUE PINS CLEARLY DOMINATE THE REST OF THE MAP. Those are Dad's. He's the only one who has pins on each of the seven continents. Mom comes in at a close second. She's only missing Antarctica. Dad was only able to visit because he was working in Argentina, his tenth pin in South America, and while there, he hopped on a boat to Antarctica.

Dad has the coolest job ever. He travels the world to collect art pieces from different museums and then arranges for their shipping to Boston, where the pieces are displayed at the Museum of Fine Arts, or what we call the MFA. That's why, today, we're both traveling to France. I'll be helping him inspect and bring over art for the new *Kings and*

Queens of the World exhibit. And, as a plus, I'll get my third pin.

Dad claims my unborn brother is in third place on the pin count. Since Mom was already pregnant when she visited Japan, Thailand, and the Philippines to study conservation practices of Asian art, my unborn brother can technically claim four pins on the wall. His pins are going to be green. When we bought the pins, Dad joked he would place them on the wall once my brother's born. I *will* challenge the motion and ask that the count begins at birth.

Eager to get my pin on the wall, I close the book on my lap, rub my eyes, and jump out of the armchair I've been reading in for the past hour. I'm not supposed to be awake yet. Mom especially doesn't like it when I get in trouble before the sun comes up. But I couldn't go back to sleep after the nightmare I had in which I missed my flight to France. It woke me up, and I've been reading ever since. I glance at the clock on Dad's desk. It's almost 6:00 A.M. Well . . . it's 5:35 A.M., to be exact. That makes it five minutes closer to six than to five. Seems like a good time to go and wake my parents.

3

I TIPTOE TO MY PARENTS' BEDROOM. ALL IS SILENT. Except for Dad's snoring. So scratch that. Everything is *noisy*. Deafening. I honestly don't understand how Mom can sleep with such a racket going on. I tiptoe around the bed to reach Dad's side.

"Dad," I whisper as I kneel next to the bed. A loud snore is his only response. "Dad," I say, a little bit louder.

Mom shifts around on the other side of the bed, still asleep. She moves slowly. She's become slower and slower ever since her belly got bigger and bigger. Sometimes I think if I prick her with a needle, my baby brother will just pop out, and I won't have to wait another couple of weeks for his arrival.

"Dad." But still he doesn't open his eyes. I'm worried we won't make our flight, so I lift up one of his eyelids and yell, "We're going to miss our flight, Dad!"

That gets him out of bed.

"Julieta, run and get your bag," he says as he searches for his pants. "Honey," he tells Mom, "wake up. Julieta and I are leaving." Mom simply grunts and rolls over to her other side.

When he finds his pants, he begins putting them on over his pajamas. His hair has the biggest cowlick I've ever seen. That, and the fact that he starts jumping on his left leg, trying to fit his right leg into the pants, make me giggle.

"What is going on?" Mom's waking up now. She struggles to prop herself up on the bed as Dad switches legs. Mom reaches for the cell phone on her nightstand, her long dark-brown hair cascading in waves over her shoulders as she leans over. "Manuel, stop jumping. It's not even six in the morning."

Dad stops struggling mid-jump and slumps back onto the bed. "Julieta," he says slowly. "Go back to bed."

"Dad, I can't do that. You said we're leaving at seven. Hurry up. We're gonna miss our flight."

Dad puts his head between his hands.

"Corazón." Mom gestures for me to come over. "You're not leaving until 7:00 P.M., not A.M."

"I know that." I sit next to her on the bed. "But what if there's traffic? Or a long line at the airport? You always say how the TSA gets worse every day."

Dad sighs. "I'll tell you what we'll do. If you let us go back to bed, we'll leave for the airport with more than enough time."

I weigh my limited options and respond. "Impossible. I can't go back to sleep now. Counteroffer." Mom and I bargain all the time, and usually I get pretty good deals, so maybe it will work with Dad, too. "I take a shower and read and come back promptly at seven."

"Eight." Dad drives a tough bargain.

"Seven thirty. Final offer."

"Deal." He smiles.

Happy with the deal I brokered, I run out of my room. I adjust the alarm on my watch to 7:30 A.M. and head to the bathroom to take a shower.

After getting dressed, I kneel in front of my bookcase and thumb through my collection, searching for a book that will keep me occupied until Mom and Dad wake up. Water drips onto my shoulders. I should have dried my hair a little more carefully.

After considering all the titles on my bookcase, I give up and go back to my parents' study. My Greek mythology book keeps calling to me. I'm going to switch it up a bit and read about the coolest goddess of them all, Athena.

Athena is probably the smartest of all the gods because she was born out of Zeus's forehead. I don't know everything about "the birds and the bees," as Dad refers to the topic, but I do know that stepping out of someone's head is not how babies are born. And I'm sure my baby brother is not sprouting from Mom's forehead. Anyway, back to Athena.

Not only is Athena the smartest goddess in Greek mythology, she's also a brave warrior. She was the mastermind behind the killing of Medusa, the snake-haired gorgon who could turn people to stone if they looked into her eyes. Athena knew her half brother Perseus would turn into stone if he looked directly at her, so she gave him a mirror shield to let him see where Medusa was without actually looking into her eyes.

The plan worked, 'cause Perseus chopped off her head.

4

AT 7:28 A.M. I'M STANDING OUTSIDE THE DOOR TO MY parents' bedroom. It stands ajar. Mom is sitting on the edge of the bed while Dad kneels in front of her, rubbing her feet. I don't go in. It would be a breach of the deal I made with him. But from where I'm standing, I can see the back of his head and the little bit of balding that's been happening for the last year. I don't usually get to see it, because he's so tall, but now that he's kneeling, the shiny spot surrounded by his curly black hair pulls at my focus. Mom said not to mention it to him. Apparently it's a sore subject.

"Who's going to do this for you while I'm gone?" Dad asks Mom.

"I'll be fine," she answers. "If they get extremely

swollen . . ." She pauses for a couple seconds. "I guess I'll just have to walk to the corner store and ask Don Armando to rub them for me."

Dad drops a foot. "Erica, I'm serious." His low voice gets harder to hear. "I'll let Dr. Jenkins know I can't go anymore. He'll have to arrange everything without me. Any other handler could bring the MFA's articles back."

Dr. Jenkins is the head of the museum. I like him. He has a big jar filled with bite-sized candy in his office, and he always lets me grab two pieces when I visit.

"Manuel, you can't do that," Mom says. "They're making cuts. Please don't give him any *more* reasons to fire you. Julieta's—let's call it *feat*—already has you and me both on thin ice."

Mom must be referring to last week's incident. I had been walking through the MFA's Impressionism halls when it happened. I noticed one of the paintings was a tiny bit crooked. Naturally, I tried to fix it. However, I tilted it a little too much, and an alarm went off as it slid down to the floor. The canvas wasn't damaged, but the corner of the frame split. Mom was called over to analyze the damage, since she heads the museum's art conservation department, *and* because she's usually the judge on how much of a punishment I get. Thankfully, she'll be leading the frame's repair once her maternity leave is over.

I had never seen Dr. Jenkins so angry. He huffed and puffed as he walked the length of his office over and over, never saying a word.

It was the first time I left his office without any candy.

My watch beeps. 7:30 A.M. Time to go!

5

"LET'S GO, LET'S GO, LET'S GO! WE'RE BURNING daylight here. We need to hurry. We'll miss our flight!" I say as I swing the door wide open.

Mom and Dad smile at each other, and Mom says, "First, breakfast." Ever since she started eating for two, she's hyper-focused on meals.

"Fine, just a quick bite. But we have to hurry after that."

"I'll have to make a stop at the museum before we go to the airport," Dad says. "There are some things I have to take care of before we leave."

A visit to the museum and a trip halfway around the world. This day is getting better by the minute.

After breakfast, I brush my teeth as fast as I can

and roll my luggage to the door. Mom helps Dad finish his packing. Finally, we walk downstairs, where a taxi waits for us.

"Wait! I forgot to pack a book to read on the plane," I say.

Dad lets out an exaggerated sigh. "I thought you didn't want to miss the flight," he says as I run up the front steps.

"I'll be back in less than a minute," I yell back. "One, two, three . . ." I count as I climb the stairs. We live on the second floor, so I don't have to wait for the elevator or run up five flights of stairs.

I'm up to fifteen seconds when I reach our floor. Turning the corner to our hallway, I bump into Robin. She sometimes "babysits" me. Or that's what we tell Mom and Dad. Secretly, we've agreed I'm too old for babysitting, and we can just call each other friends who hang out together.

"Hi, Julieta! Where's the fire?" she asks with a smile.

"No fire," I tell her. "Today is the day!" I've been telling her about going to France with Dad since I heard about it three weeks ago.

"Cool beans," she says and puts a hand up high

for me. Although Robin is a very serious clinical psychology student, she sometimes says the funniest phrases. I take a couple steps back, sprint, and jump up to return the high five, laughing. Even though she's not too tall, a year ago I wasn't able to reach it. Maybe in the fall, once I start fifth grade, I'll be able to reach it without the running start.

"Nice. So when are you leaving?" she asks.

"Right now," I tell her, "but I forgot a book for the plane."

"Run, then. And have a great trip!"

I rush into the apartment and kneel in front of the bookcase in my room. I think about grabbing *The Invention of Hugo Cabret*, since it's set in France, but it's very heavy. Besides, Mom and I have been reading it together before going to bed, and I don't want to read ahead without her. Instead, I grab *Matilda*. As I walk by the study, I remember I left my mythology book in there. I pick it up, too. It's always better to have more than one book on a trip. Then I run back down the stairs.

6

Mom is counting as I open the door to the street. "Fifty-seven, fifty-eight, fifty-nine."

"I'm here!" I jump down the last three steps and land with a *thump* on the sidewalk.

"Wow!" Dad says. "Just under one minute. You are indeed very fast."

I know it took me longer than a minute, so I wink at him. He winks back and turns to Mom. "If all goes well, we'll be gone for six days," he says, holding her by the shoulders. "That gives us another week before the official due date."

He kisses her on the forehead, and she stands on tiptoe to kiss him on the lips. Smiling, he kneels to kiss her tummy and says, "And you, sin salir de ahí todavía.

Please wait to exit the womb until we come back." He stands again to hug her.

Mom smiles. "If this one turns out like Julieta, he won't wait that long."

She turns and hugs me tight. I can barely breathe. "I got you something for your trip," she says, releasing me, and takes a charm bracelet out of her pocket. "You can collect one from every place you visit. And as you can see, I already added the first one, so you can remember home."

As she clasps the bracelet around my wrist, I see the difference in our skin color. I love that she has lighter skin and Dad has darker skin. Me, I'm in the happy middle ground between the two.

Once Mom is done fastening the bracelet, I turn it over to see a tiny swan from the Public Garden. "Gracias, Mamá!"

"I'll miss you both. Take care of your dad, sweetie, and help him out by staying out of trouble." She squeezes me again.

"I will, Mom!" I say, struggling to breathe. She loosens her grip a little, but I hug her back before she lets go.

Dad and I get into the cab. "The MFA, please," he tells the driver.

After a few moments of silence, I turn to Dad. "He won't be born before we come back, right?" I ask. "He'll wait for us?"

Dad looks up from the sheet of paper he was reading. "Who'll wait for us?"

"My baby brother."

Dad puts his hand on my shoulder. "The baby will come whenever he needs to come. And if everything goes as planned, we'll be there when he does."

"I just want to be the first person he meets," I say. "I've been waiting for him for nine years." *And verbally asking for a brother or sister since I could form coherent sentences.*

"I know, Julieta." He wraps his arm around me and squeezes. "In the meantime, how about we think up more names for him?"

Dad and I both love this game.

"Perseus . . . Apollo . . . Ares . . ." I love Greek mythology.

"Re . . . Seth . . . Amun . . ." Dad loves Egyptian mythology.

We both laugh because we know my brother's name will be Antonio, like Mom's dad. She already decided. Still, Dad and I have fun playing the game.

Before I realize it, we've arrived at the MFA. The cab driver leaves us at the employee entrance. Dad grabs the luggage from the taxi as I use his ID card to open the door to my favorite place in the city.

7

As soon as we walk into the museum, I feel at home. If I could spend all my time here, I would. I used to visit more with Mom, but Dad could only manage to bring me sometimes. Now he lets me tag along to work with him if he's sure I'll have adult supervision while wandering through the amazing halls.

The floors in the office hallways squeak with every step I take. I start skipping. *Squeak, squeakin', squeak, squeakity.*

"I have to pick up some files from my office and meet with Dr. Jenkins before we go to the airport," Dad says. He opens the door to the hallway that leads to the administration offices. "Why don't you go and visit *Athena* in the meantime?"

I stare at him and squint, trying to figure out if this is some kind of test. I thought I wasn't allowed to roam the galleries on my own.

"It's okay," he tells me. "I'm trusting you this time. I *can* trust you, right?"

I nod and turn to walk the other way, toward the galleries. After a couple of steps, I turn back, expecting him to tell me it was all a joke, and I have to wait seated in his office without uttering a single word.

"Go ahead," he says. "I'll come and get you once I'm done."

Before he changes his mind, I turn and head down the hallway leading to the gallery that holds *Athena*.

Athena Parthenon, as she is officially named, is probably my favorite piece in the whole museum. First of all, it's Greek. And I do love anything Greek. Second, I'm really into Athena as a god right now. Not only was she wise, but Zeus also trusted her with his thunderbolt and the aegis, a special shield. Finally, the statue's missing its arms. And that's the best thing about old statues, especially Greek and Roman old statues. My parents and I have gotten into a tradition of posing with statues missing a head or limb. Athena was the first in the series. I posed behind the statue with my arms out. Mom always says the missing pieces are a part of history that's lost forever. Wars, natural disasters, transportation, or the simple passage of time are all causes for loss. But that's why I like them the best — they've been around for quite some time.

On our last visit to the Met Museum in New York, my parents and I posed with the statue of *The Three Graces*. That statue shows three women, Aglaea, Euphrosyne, and Thalia — all handmaidens to Aphrodite, the goddess of love and beauty, all daughters of Zeus (the guy has about a bajillion children), and all headless. They weren't decapitated or anything; the heads of the statue just got broken off at some point in history. "A casualty of time," Mom says.

Mom, Dad, and I took a picture posing with each one of us as a head. Mom and Dad were tall enough that their heads showed over the necks. I, on the other hand, needed to stand on a stool. When we printed out the picture in Dad's office, we laughed for hours. We hadn't realized it until then, but the body of the middle Grace is turned around. With my head facing the same way as my parents, it looks like it has a life of its own. A copy of the picture sits on my nightstand.

I feel a pang in my stomach. I wish Mom could join us on our trip. I'm sure we'll find many headless statues at the Louvre.

I push that thought out of my head and decide to focus instead on the beauty around me. The museum halls are empty, since it hasn't opened yet. It takes all my willpower not to run all the way to the gallery where *Athena* is located. Instead, I speed-walk, moving my arms just like people do in the Olympics—which, interestingly, started in Ancient Greece. I take all the right turns and shortcuts. But just before I make the turn that will lead me to the Ancient World section, a veiled entrance to a different gallery catches my eye. I skid to a stop.

8

"SCREECH!" I BLURT OUT, SINCE I FEEL IT'S NECESSARY to voice the sound effect.

Behind the curtains lies the home to the new exhibit Dad and his team are preparing. Velvet ropes stand in front of the covered entrance. Hanging from one of them is a plastic sign that reads: *KINGS AND QUEENS OF THE WORLD* EXHIBIT UNDER CONSTRUCTION. AUTHORIZED PERSONNEL ONLY BEYOND THIS POINT.

Technically I'm personnel, right? I'm part of the team that's putting the exhibit together. This helps me feel a little less guilty when I pull the fabric aside and enter the room.

The room is dimly lit, and it takes my eyes a few seconds to adjust. Scaffolds and plastic covers are all over the place. I can see the partitions they've built in the room with their vinyl signs indicating where the art from each of the six kingdoms will be showcased. The Incan empire from Peru. Egypt and its pharaohs. China and its mighty dynasties. The Mongol empire and the Great Khan. The Persian Empire of old. And last but not least, France and its royal sovereigns. The last is where the art pieces and jewelry Dad and I will pick up in France will be located.

I walk with my hands behind my back, trying not to touch anything, just like I promised Dad. But I climb up a scaffold to have a better look at the hall. I don't remember him specifying anything about climbing, so I figure it's okay.

The scaffold wobbles a little. I hold steady and try not to look down. I make it to the top after a few more rungs. At the top I lie down on my stomach and look out at the big hall. The room is silent. I close my eyes and try to picture all the statues, paintings, and jewels that will soon fill the space.

In my mind King Tut's golden mask sits in the middle of the room, surrounded by lit torches. I'm sure King Midas would have loved that mask. Paintings hang on most of the walls, and a suit of armor guards the exhibit's entrance.

The suit of armor turns around to look at me. Its whole body creaks. Clearly, it is in desperate need of some oil. It raises its hand. More creaking. I can't stop looking at its hand, from which a very bright jewel is dangling and reflecting the light from the torches suddenly lit all over the room. The helmet's visor moves up and down, as if trying to mouth a word. A soft "Julieta" leaks from the opening.

"Julieta . . . Julieta . . . Juuulieeetaa." My name is the only word coming from the suit of armor, and it seems to be getting louder and louder. This can't be real. Can it?

9

"JULIETA!"

I open my eyes and see Dad calling for me from the bottom of the scaffold. I sit up and realize I'd dozed off and had been dreaming. There are no lit torches. With a sigh of relief, I notice the suit of armor *is* there, but standing against the wall, like the stillest of guards. Its visor is tightly shut.

"What are you doing up there? I've been looking all over the museum for you. We're leaving right after I talk to Dr. Jenkins," Dad demands.

I stare at him, getting the fuzz out of my head.

"Are you coming? Or would you rather just stay here napping instead of going to France?"

"I'm coming, I'm coming," I blurt out. "I'll be down

in a second! Don't leave without me!" I hurry down the scaffold, but miss the last step and take a tumble. I look up from the floor. Dad's standing there, his hands on his hips. He glares down on me. I grin up at him.

"Julieta, please be more careful," Dad pleads. "You could've hurt yourself. And I thought I told you not to touch anything."

"But I didn't! Not really." I stand up and ceremoniously wipe dust from my pants. It's the only excuse I can give. I know he's mad at me, but I still reach up and give him a kiss on the cheek. He starts to smile.

"Come on. No breaking stuff around the exhibit before it opens. At least give us a fighting chance." He sighs as he heads back toward the offices. I hurry after him.

When we reach Dr. Jenkins's office, Dad asks, "Would you mind hanging out here?"

"Sure," I say. "Is Joanna around?"

Joanna is one of Dr. Jenkins's assistants. She just graduated with her master's degree in art history and will soon be traveling to Peru and other South American countries to study Incan art. I wonder how many pins would be on her world map. When I grow up, I want to travel like Dad and Joanna, looking at and touching ancient art. However, if I can help it, I'll spend most of my time in Greece.

"I didn't see her around," Dad says. "She might be at a meeting."

"That's okay," I tell him. "I know where she keeps the cards."

Joanna has been teaching me how to play solitaire whenever I visit the museum. She keeps a deck of cards just for me in one of her drawers. They are Piet Mondrian–themed: all white, red, yellow, and blue squares with black lines. So as soon as Dad walks into Dr. Jenkins's office, I sit down at Joanna's desk and take out the deck stashed in the bottom drawer. I quickly set up the game and focus on getting my aces. "The aces are the basis for a good solitaire game," Joanna told me once.

I'm halfway through the game when Joanna walks into the room. Her long and flowy skirt swishes with her big steps. A pencil sticks out of her high bun. She seems flustered and a bit confused. Maybe she can't find her pencil.

"Julieta! I didn't know you were here. How are you doing? Is your dad here? How about Dr.

Jenkins?" she asks without taking a breath or letting me answer.

"They're in a meeting together," I say, pointing at the door.

"Great, they're both here." Without waiting for them to come out, or even knocking on the door, Joanna rushes into Dr. Jenkins's office. "The museum must remain closed," she announces. "There's a piece missing."

10

STARTLED BY HER DECLARATION, I RUSH INTO THE office as well. Dad and Dr. Jenkins are sitting on a couch, clearly stunned. Even though the couch could comfortably sit three people, Dr. Jenkins is so much taller and bigger than Dad that it seems Dad is crouching at the end of the couch.

"Which piece?" Dr. Jenkins asks in his deep voice.

Joanna looks at her notes. "The accession number for the piece is 03.990. It's the small bronze statuette of Athena. The one with the empty hands. The *Promachos*."

I know the piece Joanna is referring to. It always grabbed my attention because her hands aren't just bare, but actually emptied out. I asked Dad about it when I first noticed it, and he helped me search the museum's records. A spear and an owl are believed to be missing from her hands. Once more, a part of a statue was lost in time.

"One of the attendants on the floor was doing her rounds this morning and noticed the empty case where the piece had been displayed," Joanna continued.

"Julieta." Dad turns to me. "You were in the rooms earlier today. Did you happen to *borrow* it when you were in there?"

His accusatory tone as he says "borrow" hurts my pride. Why would he ask if I took it? Right, 'cause I *borrowed* a coin once when I was six years old. Three years and a broken frame later, I know I'm absolutely and utterly not supposed to touch any of the pieces, but I still can't seem to live it down. "Don't touch anything but the floor," Dad had said in the aftermath of the "incident."

Both Joanna and Dad are staring at me, expecting me to admit I took the statuette. I've spent a lot of time in that room, but I never even made it to the Greek wing this morning.

Dr. Jenkins clears his throat and runs his fingers through his light-brown hair. "Manuel, Joanna, stop accusing the child."

I sigh in relief. Dr. Jenkins to the rescue. Wait, how does he know I didn't take it?

"This time it's my fault," he continues. "The head of the history and architecture department at Boston University called me yesterday evening. One of their grad students wrote a surprisingly creative article on the statue conceptualizing what she could have held in her hands. He requested to take some pictures of it for the article. I came back, but you had already left, Joanna, so I had it moved to the labs for cleaning before he comes next week to take the pictures."

"Where's the movement request form?" Joanna asks. "I didn't see it in the log this morning."

"It must still be on my desk," Dr. Jenkins admits, pointing to a pile of documents that look uninteresting. "I'll get it to you later today."

Joanna doesn't seem convinced, but nods. "I'll confirm with the lab and get credentials for the student." She walks out of the room. Nobody has dismissed me yet, so to avoid any other accusations, I stay standing next to the door.

Dad turns to me and mouths, *Sorry*.

I smile in reply. I understand why he jumped

to conclusions. My record at the museum isn't the cleanest.

Dr. Jenkins stands up and walks to his desk, opens my favorite jar, and tosses a piece of candy to me. I catch it with ease.

"Thanks," I tell him, looking at the peace offering. This must mean he forgives me for messing up the frame last week.

"Anytime," he says. "You know you're my favorite of all the Leal clan."

I smile at him and leave his office to find Joanna sitting at her desk. "Sorry, kiddo," she says. "Didn't mean to blame you."

I shrug and say, "We're cool, but I need your help finishing my game."

After about ten minutes, I finish my round of solitaire. Joanna helped for a bit but got called away.

Dad and Dr. Jenkins finally walk out of the office. "Remember," Dr. Jenkins says, "there's no room for error. Not on this trip, Manuel."

Dad looks at me before shaking Dr. Jenkins's hand. "There will be none."

11

WE ARRIVE AT THE AIRPORT AND CHECK OUR BAGS. Our flight doesn't leave for some hours yet, so after we pass through security, we walk around the airport and window-shop at the gift shops and bookstores. The wait is torture. I think I visit every single shop in our terminal at least three times. But that doesn't make time go by any faster. It only makes my feet hurt from walking all around the airport. When it's finally time to board, we make our way to the international departure gates.

"Welcome, and have a good flight," says one of the flight attendants standing at the airplane door.

"We're going to Paris!" I beam at her.

"I see that. Make sure to try the escargots."

I'm so confused I stop walking. Scarred goats. At least that's what I think she's saying. Am I supposed to eat them or pet them? Before I can ask any follow-up questions about how the goats get injured and developed scars, Dad pushes me forward to find our seats.

"I wish the aisle was a little wider," I tell Dad as I struggle to avoid bumping my bag into the seats on each side.

"No, you don't," he says. "Otherwise the seats would have to be smaller. And that would be bad, especially when you have to fly for seven hours straight."

He does have a point. I'm grateful when we make it to our seats and put our carry-on luggage away. I can't reach the overhead compartment, so Dad helps me lift my bag.

"This will be the best trip ever," I say. "We'll see the Eiffel Tower, and the gardens at Versailles, and eat croissants, and—"

He smiles. "Just buckle your seat belt. We're taking off soon."

After we get all the safety instructions for the flight, I turn to the window to see the airplane slowly moving on the tarmac. We finally make our way to the runway. I look over at Dad. "Hey, Dad."

He's sound asleep. His breathing is slow and deep. How is it possible for him to sleep with so much excitement? I, on the other hand, am completely wired. We've only been waiting a few minutes to take off, but I'm already getting bored. I wish I could walk up and down the aisle. Dad was smart by "letting me" have the window seat. This way he has me locked in. *Touché, old man, touché*. In defeat, I keep my eyes on the window.

"Okay, folks," I hear over the intercom. "We're next for takeoff. We hope you have a pleasant flight. Our estimated flight time will be . . ."

The plane quickly picks up speed. After a few seconds I feel the front of the plane lift. Soon all that's left to see from the window is the ocean. Blue—it's all blue. Just blue and some white foam from the waves. But soon that disappears too as we climb through the clouds.

I turn back to Dad, who's now snoring. Nothing too loud yet. This is going to be a long flight.

Thankfully, the seat in front of me has a touchscreen on the back of the headrest. I start fiddling around with it, tapping through to find something to watch. After a few minutes, I find an old movie called *The*

Mummy. It has ancient Egyptian tombs, lost artifacts, and disgusting beetles. I want to see how accurate this depiction is of ancient Egypt, so I plug in the headphones provided in the seatback pocket and click PLAY.

Dad jostles me awake.

"Chicken or beef?" the flight attendant asks with her cart of dinner trays.

How much time has gone by?

"Do you have any spaghetti?" I ask, half asleep.

She laughs. "I'll go to the back and see what I can find for you, sweetie."

Dad is already digging into his dinner. I peek and see it's the chicken dish, then look out the window and discover it's night already. "Dad, how come it got dark outside so quickly? Are we all the way up in space?"

"We're going west to east, through many time zones. Paris is a few time zones ahead, so it's much later there right now."

"So it's like we're going into the future?" I ask, amazed.

"Kind of, but it's more about where the Earth is compared to the sun. It's all happening at the same time. We just see the sun at different times."

I'm still imagining the world speeding and spinning through space when the flight attendant returns with a pasta plate. Penne marinara. Not spaghetti, but I'll take it. "Thank you," I tell her.

"Sure, sweetie," she says. "Let me know if you're still hungry after that. And if you get cold . . ." She points to the pillow and blanket I've smushed against the window.

The pasta is okay, but I wish it had less sauce, because I spilled some on my shirt. Dad gets me a new T-shirt out of my bag and says, "You know we won't have twenty-four-hour access to a laundromat."

After dinner I use the bathroom to change and quickly brush my teeth. Bathrooms on airplanes are tiny, and if you're not careful when you flush, you might get swallowed by the blue liquid in the toilet. I return to my seat, ready to share this thought with Dad, but he's asleep again. I tuck myself into a little ball and try to sleep as well.

12

IT'S ALREADY MORNING WHEN THE PLANE TOUCHES ground in France.

Paris, here I come.

I make a mental note to call Mom as soon as possible and ask her to add another purple pin to the map.

After going through Customs, we walk toward baggage claim and see a tall, thin mustached man holding a white cardboard that says: MONSIEUR ET MADEMOISELLE LEAL. He introduces himself as Jacques Legrand. To my disappointment, his blond mustache doesn't curl up at the ends like in the movies.

"I'm with the Louvre. I'm the assistant to Dr. Srivas, the registrar," he tells Dad as he rubs the mustache. "We spoke on the phone a couple of times?"

"Yes. It's great to put a face to the voice," Dad says. He shakes Jacques's hand. "How are you doing?"

"Fine, thank you," Jacques says. "We have a car waiting for you when you're ready."

Dad and I video-call Mom while we wait for our bags to come out on the conveyor belt.

"Bonjour, mademoiselle. How's Paris?" she asks when her beautiful face comes up on the screen. Her smile is as warm as always. It's wide enough that it makes the skin around her eyes crinkle a bit. Another pang in my stomach. I'm pretty far away from the best hugger in the world.

"I don't know yet. I haven't been out of the airport, but I am already in France. So . . ."

"Right," she says, putting a purple pin within the camera's view. "Straight to business with you."

After I see the purple pin is properly pinned on the map and Mom reminds us to visit the Sacré-Cœur church, we hang up. Then I turn my attention to Jacques.

He's taller than Dad and maybe older. My hunch about his age seems right when he takes off his hat and I can see he's bald. He has way less hair than Dad. However, I think his mustache makes up for the hair missing on the top of his head. I wonder if the blindingly bright blue gum he is chewing with determination has ever gotten stuck on his mustache. That would be a pain to take out. Although Mom used lemon oil when I got some Hubba Bubba Bubble Tape gum stuck in my hair.

"Can I have some gum?" I ask Jacques.

"Je suis désolé, chérie," he tells me. "I'm sorry. This is nicotine gum. To help me stop smoking."

Outside the terminal Jacques points to a van that says LOUVRE on the side. We climb into the van, and I find a young woman already in the passenger seat. She looks a bit like Jacques with the same green eyes but with blonder—and way more—hair. On her head, not her face.

"Alors, let me introduce to you to Monique, my daughter," Jacques tells Dad and me. "We'll both be helping you out during your stay in France, Monsieur Leal."

"You're working at the museum?" I ask Monique.

"Oui." Monique switches from the passenger's seat to the backseat with me. "I'm helping my father during the summer. For now, I'm doing ticketing, but I'll hopefully work in one of the exhibits by the end of the summer, when I turn sixteen."

"You're fifteen and working at the museum? That's amazing," I almost yell. I'm shocked she's fifteen, since I'm almost as tall as her. "Hopefully I'll get to be that lucky when I'm older."

"I'm sure you will. Ask your father if you can be his assistant," she says. "That would be a good place to start."

"Dad won't let me help much around the museum. He says I'm a liability." I whisper the last part.

"I don't know that word in English. What does it mean?"

"I don't really know the *exact* meaning." I scratch my head. "But it must have something to do with me almost breaking one of the Egyptian burial vases last year . . . and a painting's frame a couple of weeks ago."

Even though Monique tries to stifle a laugh, it comes out as a snort. I'm glad she finds that amusing. Most people look a little horrified after I tell them that piece of information. Sometimes they even clutch whatever they are holding closer. As if I go around grabbing everything and throwing it on the floor.

"You must be hungry," Jacques says. "I don't know about you, but I'm not really a fan of airplane food."

Jacques and Monique take us to a café to have

some breakfast before touring Paris. The restaurant is very small, but it has a lot of tables outside on the street. Next to our table, there's an old lady with a huge French poodle having some coffee and a croissant. France must have her sitting there just for the tourists' benefit.

After my delicious cheese omelet and a pain au chocolat—or a chocolate-stuffed delight, as I will now call it—I'm convinced the French clearly know their way around a kitchen. I can't wait to taste everything they have to offer. I'm also grateful I slept on the plane ride, because there's so much to see in Paris.

13

WE BEGIN OUR TOUR BY GOING TO THE ARC DE Triomphe. Jacques puts the van in park on a side street and drops Monique, Dad, and me off. I jump out and hurry toward the arch. But as I get closer, I'm unsure if I want to attempt going all the way there. The arch stands at the center of a roundabout with cars constantly driving around it. To my surprise and relief, Monique leads Dad and me to an underground passage pedestrians use to reach the other side of the street. I'm not even a day in, and I'm already discovering the secrets of Paris.

On the other side of the tunnel, the arch awaits us. I stand in the center and look up. It's massive.

Dad stands next to me and asks, "Do you want to climb some stairs?"

"We can go up?"

After we climb the two hundred and eighty-four steps, I have to admit I'm a little out of breath. However, I'm pleased to discover it's totally worth it.

Down below, twelve streets flow into the giant roundabout surrounding the arch. All the cars are speeding around in the same direction, in and out of the busy streets, like they're heading into unavoidable crashes. Parisians must be great drivers if they can avoid any accidents in this roundabout with seemingly no rules.

Once I'm able to pull my attention from the cars below, I am even more awed by the view of the city. Some streets end in gardens.

"The Champs-Elysées," Monique informs me, pointing to one large street. "And at the end, there's another arch. But it's a lot smaller."

If I look to the right, I can also see the Eiffel Tower from here. "Let's go there next," I tell Dad.

Once back in the car, we enter the roundabout ourselves and then cross a bridge over the Seine River. Finally, we arrive at what I consider to be the main attraction: the Eiffel Tower. I leap out of the car and head toward the elevator.

"Julieta, wait! We need tickets to go up," Dad yells after me.

I stop in my tracks and turn around. When Dad and Monique catch up with me, I take Dad's hand, and we walk to the tower. He purchases tickets, and we head to an elevator. I'm thankful I won't have to climb all the way up. After the Arc de Triomphe, my legs are a bit tired.

"Take us to the highest floor," I beg the elevator's attendant as Dad, Monique, and I climb inside.

"The tower is one hundred and eight stories high, miss," he says.

"Take us up," I answer as quickly as possible. Dad stares. "Please," I add.

The attendant closes the gates of the elevator, and we start moving up fast.

"Have you ever been up here?" I ask Monique.

"Just once," she says, tying her blonde hair in a ponytail. "But I was younger than you are right now, so I'm glad I get to visit again."

When we reach the second floor, the elevator gates open. "To reach the highest floor you must switch elevators," the attendant informs us.

We switch elevators and when I'm at the top of the tower, I can see all of Paris. "Dad, what direction is Boston?" I ask.

"West from here, so that way." He points behind me.

I know it's a whole ocean away, but still, I blow a kiss in Mom's general direction and yell, "Te extraño!"

Dad joins in. "I miss you too, Erica."

Back down at the gift shop, Dad and I look for a souvenir for my soon-to-be baby brother. "I think we should get him a keychain," Dad suggests.

"But he won't use keys for about ten years. *I* don't even have keys." Sometimes Dad doesn't really think things through.

"How about a snow globe?" he asks.

We get two snow globes—one the size of my head for Mom, the other the teeniest, tiniest, cutest one for Antonio. Dad also buys a charm for my bracelet. It's a tiny version of the Eiffel Tower.

"See," he tells me. "You already have two!"

I smile and hug him.

That evening, Jacques and Monique drop us off at the hotel. "We'll be here early tomorrow," Jacques tells us. "The Louvre is our first stop."

14

AFTER AN EARLY BREAKFAST, WE RUSH BACK UPSTAIRS to brush our teeth. Soon after, Monique and Jacques pick us up in the Louvre van. I'm excited to head to the Louvre, where we'll be looking at the pieces we'll borrow and take back to Boston with us. Plus, we'll get to inspect other objects, which the Louvre will send with its own handler. Like, a supposedly cursed diamond will be the main attraction in the exhibit. Even though I would love to travel with a diamond in our bags, special and valuable objects are transported by the museum that owns them.

When we arrive, I can't help but admire the glass pyramid, which is probably the most famous entrance to the Louvre. It also has one of the longest lines I've ever seen in my entire life. Thankfully, since we're on official museum business, we're able to skip the line. A museum guard escorts us to the offices. To my dismay, I don't even get to glimpse the *Mona Lisa*, Leonardo da Vinci's most famous work.

"We can ask to come back when the museum is closed," Dad says when he notices my disappointment. "You probably wouldn't even be able to look at it right now. It's always crowded. I would need to lift you up on my shoulders for you to get a decent look."

I look at Monique. I hope she didn't hear that. Only little girls are carried by their dads on their shoulders. If Monique finds out Dad gave me a lift at a concert a couple of months ago, she might think I'm too young to be Dad's assistant.

"I can wait," I say.

I also think this is what Mom would want me to do. Before leaving I promised Mom I'd help Dad. If she were here, she'd tell me, "Mucho ayuda el que no estorba." That means helping by not being in the way. I plan to keep that promise, no matter what it takes. That is why I won't even ask to explore the museum on my own. I'll wait, patiently seated in a chair, and come back later when I get to touch the art. Actually, scratch that. I've turned over a new leaf, and I won't even touch the art. No matter how pretty it is, or how squishy the paint looks.

We all climb into the elevator, which is tiny. I'm thankful when Monique and Jacques leave us after a couple of floors to do some work of their own. The last stop on the elevator is the lab floor.

After exiting, we are taken to the room where the artwork for the *Kings and Queens of the World* exhibit is being stored. As I walk in, the first thought that comes to mind is that this must be what Ali Baba's cave looked like. The room is filled with interesting objects. Light glitters all over. Wooden crates are placed next to stainless steel tables with different art pieces on them.

The MFA back home owns some really cool pieces, but this collection is impressive. And the pieces in this room are the ones the Louvre will be loaning out to other museums. I see a golden goblet with jewels encrusted on it. Wooden chairs stand next to another open crate. Personally, I don't understand why adults get so excited about chairs. Maybe it's because older people are tired most of the time and look forward to the prospect of sitting down. Either way, I have to admit the chairs are beautiful. They have complicated designs on the backrest, the legs, and the arms. The seats are covered with bright red velvet. As I look closely I can see the velvet is worn out. That's a sign of a very old chair, I've learned. A rolled-up rug also stands next to another tall, thin crate. Maybe it's a magic carpet. I can't wait to spread it out.

The table in the middle of the room is blocked from my view by a short woman who turns when we walk in. She is wearing a yellow-and-pink sari that contrasts with her dark blue lab coat.

"Welcome, Monsieur Leal!" she says to my dad. "My name is Dr. Miriam Srivas. I'm the Louvre's head registrar. I'll be inspecting the art pieces with you before we pack and ship them to the United States."

Joanna once explained that the registrar is the person in charge of keeping a record of all the artwork going in and out of the museum. "It's a job with a lot of responsibilities," she told me. I'm thinking it must be a hard job to have at the Louvre. This museum is way bigger than the MFA.

I stay close to Dad as he walks up to shake her hand. "Please, call me Manuel," Dad says.

"Then I'll be Miriam." She extends her hand

toward me and says, "And you must be Julieta. Please feel free to call me Miriam as well."

"Hi, pleased to meet you," I respond. I begin to curtsy but regret it halfway because we're not in a palace, so it comes out as more of a head jerk than an elegant curtsy.

"It's great to have you here, Julieta," she says, ignoring my awkward introduction. "I'm glad you were able to tag along with your dad. I remember my art handler days. Once the art is crated, it can be boring and lonely sometimes. It's like being a babysitter who takes care of art pieces worth millions of dollars."

"But you get to visit so many places," I tell her. "I never get to go on any trips. I usually stay home with whatever parent isn't traveling or with Robin, my babysit— I mean *friend*, but since my mom is very pregnant, they thought I might be better off going on this trip."

"Are you excited to have a baby brother?"

I nod. "I've been begging my parents for a baby something ever since I can remember."

"Younger siblings are fun," she says. "I'm the oldest of six. My favorite thing is babysitting my youngest sister."

"I hope I get to babysit soon." I sigh. "Mom and Dad say I need to wait until I'm older."

"Maybe just a couple of years," Dad says. "And babies don't do much for the first couple of months anyway. You just have to be extra careful in how you handle them."

"Like art?" Uh-oh, I'll never get to babysit.

"Somewhat," Miriam says. "And about the art." She motions Dad to the table. I hang back but can still hear her say, "We've had some developments. Odette, the Louvre's handler who was scheduled to accompany the Regent Diamond, has disappeared."

15

By looking at Dad's slumped shoulders, I can immediately tell this is bad news.

"What do you mean, she disappeared?" he asks.

"About a week ago she came back from a drop in Belgium," Miriam says. "We haven't heard from her since she turned in the paperwork. That was three days ago. Unfortunately, this isn't the first time this has happened. She tends to be a little distracted, so we don't want to call the police just yet."

Dad puts his hands behind his back and paces back and forth. "And you have no one else, Dr. Srivas?" he asks, stopping in front of Miriam.

"I'm sorry, Manuel," she says apologetically. "If we had, we would have already started the paperwork.

We wanted to give her more time to see if she'd show up. But nothing so far."

Dad stands there a few more minutes.

"Of course, you'll get compensated for the extra risk of carrying the Regent with you."

"That's not it." Dad waves a hand, dismissing her. He breathes deeply a couple of times while Miriam patiently looks at him.

"Fine, I'll do it," he says. "But let's start immediately. I don't want to be here any longer than is absolutely necessary."

When Dad turns to look at me, my confusion must be clear, because he tells me, "Julieta, we'll have to stay a couple of days longer."

"Longer?" I ask. "Dad, I love Paris, but what about the baby?"

"The paperwork and inspection will take no longer than a day," Miriam assures us.

"It will be fine, Julieta," Dad says. "I have to make sure the diamond gets to the MFA as soon as possible. Security measures need to be adjusted with the actual piece before the exhibit opens."

"And almost everything is ready for you to take home," Dr. Srivas adds. "We'll check the pieces one by one. But now that you'll be responsible for it, I'm sure I know what you're the most eager to see. Why don't we start with the pièce de résistance? The Regent Diamond."

She directs us to the table in the middle of the room. The Regent Diamond has already been removed from its display case and waits, ready for us to admire it. It's been set up on a black velvet square in the middle of the table. Dad walks slowly toward it.

When he reaches the table, he puts on gloves before touching the diamond. I stay back, trying not to disturb the process.

From what I can see, the diamond is the size of a small peach, maybe an apricot. If Mom were here, she could whip out The Bump, her pregnancy tracking app. She'd probably say Antonio was that size at twelve weeks. Either way, it's a pretty big diamond.

While Dad makes sure everything checks out with the diamond, Miriam tells me, "The diamond was first worn in a crown by Louis XV."

"Was he one of the Louises who lived at Versailles?" I ask.

"Yes, one of those Louises." She chuckles. "The Regent Diamond was actually found in the Kollur Mine in India."

"India? How did it end up in Louis's crown?" I ask.

"Smuggled by a slave out of the mine, stolen by a sea captain, sold to an Indian merchant, and then again to an English governor. Finally bought by French royalty and set into the crown for Louis XV's coronation."

"Did all that really happen?" I ask, incredulous.

She chuckles again. "It truly did. It was also lost for a while during the French Revolution and hidden from the Nazis during World War II."

"If it was lost, how do you know it's the same one?" I ask, imagining the real diamond in a supervillain's secret vault.

"Its size, most importantly. But also the color, clarity, and cut. It's practically impossible to replicate this diamond, even with today's technology."

"I can't believe it survived all that," I say.

"And it might still have some more adventures in it. I understand you'll visit Versailles tomorrow?"

"Yes. Yesterday we went to the Eiffel Tower. Dad bought this for me." I raise my wrist up as high as I can so she can get a proper look at the charm on my bracelet.

"Wow," Miriam says. "That's très jolie. Very pretty."

"Thank you," I say. "Mom got me the other one. It's a swan from the botanical gardens in Boston. Do you know them?"

"I've actually visited the gardens," Miriam says. "I have a daughter who studies at MIT. When I dropped her off at school last year, we rode the swan boats. I also went to New York and saw the Statue of Liberty. France gave you that; did you know that? We have a smaller Statue of Liberty here. Have you seen it?"

I nod. "Yesterday. After the Eiffel Tower, we drove around Paris a bit. You know, you have a lot of pigeons."

Miriam laughs. "That is completely true."

"Julieta, come closer so you can see the diamond," Dad calls.

I walk toward Dad thinking I can't be surprised by anything anymore. However, when I arrive at the table, my mouth drops once more in amazement. The diamond is more beautiful up close.

"Would you like to hold the diamond?" Miriam asks.

"Yes, please!" I answer quickly, forgetting the promise I made last night.

She grabs a couple of latex gloves from a box and hands them to me. They're hard to get on, so Dad helps me. When they're on, the tips of the glove's fingers droop.

"They're a little big," I point out.

"Sorry," Miriam says. "That's the smallest size we have."

"You can sit down on that stool," Dad tells me.

I sit down and swivel so my legs are underneath the table. Miriam pushes the velvet square closer to me.

"If you hold out your hands like this"—Miriam puts her hands palms up on the table—"we'll place the diamond in them."

I lay my hands on the table, imitating her. Dad grabs the diamond and puts it in my hands. It's heavier than I expected. The diamond sparkles even brighter when Miriam moves a light directly on top of it. Gray-and-white light seems to spring from inside it. On the outside, it sparkles blue, green, red . . . all the colors of the rainbow.

"It's beautiful," I whisper, slowly putting the diamond down on its cushion, not wanting to disturb its elegance.

A loud knock comes at the door, and my reverie is broken.

16

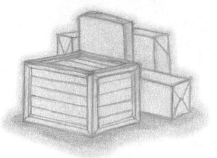

A TALL YOUNG MAN IN A GUARD'S UNIFORM IS STANDING in the doorway. He has the hairiest and craziest eyebrows I've ever seen in my life. I stifle a laugh as I notice his pants don't cover his whole leg. I can see the print on one of his socks. *Hey, that's Asterix.* Dad's favorite comic book. When Dad first shared it with me, I thought Asterix was another name for Hermes, the god of thieves and travelers. I was confused because they both have a winged helmet. I wonder if this guy's other sock has Asterix's faithful sidekick Obelix.

"Ah, Claude," Miriam says when she spots him. "Manuel, Julieta, please allow me to introduce you to Claude. He's one of the guards here at the museum. At least for the summer, right?"

Dad walks around the table to shake his hand. "It's nice to meet you, Claude."

"Nice to meet you too, sir," Claude says softly. He then turns to me. "Julieta, right?"

I nod. Why does everyone in France seem to know my name? Did someone warn the whole country I was on my way here? At least they're pronouncing Julieta with the owl's hoot.

He must have noticed my quizzical look because he says, "I'm a friend of Monique's from school. She knows I'm interested in art, so she helped me get this job. She told me to look out for you."

Ah.

He extends his hand, and I wince as soon as I touch it. I can only describe it as a moist handshake. I don't want to be rude, so I try my absolute hardest and resist drying my hand on the side of my pant leg until he turns to talk to Miriam.

"Dr. Srivas, you've got a call from the Egyptian Museum."

Miriam takes off her gloves. "Great! I've been waiting for this call," she says, walking to the exit. "Manuel, Julieta, I leave you in the most capable of hands."

Claude smiles, obviously pleased at the compliment.

"Take your time," Dad tells her. "I'll begin packing the Regent."

Claude walks closer to the table, almost cautious. "Ah, the Regent Diamond," he says. "It's taking a little trip, I understand?"

"Yes," I say. "Dad and I are escorting it back to Boston."

"Big responsibility," he tells me.

I nod, thinking about all the people trusting Dad and me to bring the diamond to Boston. Thankfully, they've already created a special case for it, so it will be protected as we travel.

"Monsieur, let me help you," Claude offers before I can ask about his socks.

Dad and Claude pack the diamond in a small box, and then they place it in a safe box embedded into one of the walls. Dad said we'd be packing everything else in crates with special seals to know if they're tampered with from the time they leave the Louvre to when they arrive at the museum in Boston. But the Regent Diamond is a special case. Dad explains that since the handler who was supposed to personally take it to Boston didn't show up, he and I will be taking its box with us when we fly back to Boston. It's the most valuable piece in the exhibit, so we'll need to keep a close watch on it.

When Miriam comes back, she joins Claude and Dad in the careful task of inspecting and packing each remaining piece. At first it's pretty boring. I sit down in a chair and watch the three of them work. I think Miriam notices I'm about to drop dead from boredom, because she hands me a pair of scissors and asks, "Julieta, would you mind helping me cut strips of bubble wrap?"

She points to a humongous bubble wrap roll. *Christmas came early!*

Julieta, I warn myself, *don't pop all the bubbles, or everything will break*. Pushing the potential broken art pieces out of my mind, I begin to cut the wrap following Miriam's instructions.

To my surprise, the rest of the inspecting and the packing goes perfectly. Usually, when I'm involved, things tend to go wrong. Not this time! Three and a half hours later, most of the crates are packed and sealed, ready for pickup in the morning. There are some boxes left, but they will be done tomorrow.

When we finish, Miriam smiles. "Manuel, I have

left instructions at the guard's desk, so you can come back tomorrow evening when the museum is closed and take a tour." She then cuts one more piece of bubble wrap and hands it to me. "To be popped at your leisure," she explains.

"Thanks," I say, and hug her. At first she seems surprised, but she returns the hug.

17

THE NEXT DAY, AFTER PACKING UP THE LAST BOXES has left us famished, Jacques and Monique drive us to a late lunch on the way to the Sacré-Cœur Basilica. Steps lead up a hill to a small plaza with more steps that go all the way up to one of the biggest churches I've ever seen. There are a couple of musicians playing with a crowd gathered around them. People are climbing up the stairs, and many more are lounging on the steps.

"Your mom wanted me to bring you here," Dad says. "There's a funicular that can take you all the way to the top, although it's a little bit slow. Do you want to walk up?"

"A funi-what?"

"Funicular, a little train that goes up the hillside," Dad explains.

I'm glad Dad made me wear sneakers today, against my wishes to wear sandals with my dress. So even though the steps seem a little intimidating, I feel like climbing up and seeing all the people hanging around. "Let's walk," I say. "I'm sure I can make it."

"You know," Dad says as we start climbing the first set of steps, "after the Basilica of Our Lady of Guadalupe in Mexico, this is your mom's favorite church."

I look around at the people lounging on the grass. People from all around the world are visiting the church. I peer up to the top to see how many steps are left. The church's three domes rise up so high, they seem to touch the sky.

I don't talk much since I'm trying to save my energy for all these steps, and for a moment, I think I'm not going to make it!

I can't help jumping up and down with my fists up high when I do reach the top—just like I saw a man do in an old movie Dad showed me once. Dad takes a picture of me.

There's music up here, but it's different than what's playing on the steps. I realize singing is coming from the church. Before I can ask who's singing, Dad points at two statues of figures on horseback, guarding the entrance. One is a woman. "Know who that woman is there?"

I shake my head.

"Saint Joan of Arc," he says. "She led the French army into battle when she was very young. A teenager."

"Right. Burned at the stake." I say solemnly. "She had visions?"

"Correct. She heard God's voice asking her to help France defeat the English during a war in the fifteenth century. She won many battles and rescued French towns. She's also carrying the crown of thorns. The possibly real crown of thorns was on display in Notre Dame, but it was moved to the Louvre after the fire in 2019."

"Seems like a lot of responsibility." I say, wondering what would happen if I had to lead an army.

As soon as we walk in, I understand why this church holds a special place in Mom's heart. People have lit hundreds of candles at the entrance, and directly above is an organ. There must be tons of pipes because the sound coming out of it is quite impressive.

I look toward the nave and see the priest is leaving

the altar. Mass is finishing up, but there are nuns still singing. "Those are Benedictine nuns," Dad whispers. "They have perpetual adoration here, so the Blessed Sacrament is out all night too."

I make a mental note to remember that Benedictine nuns wear white robes and a black veil. At home in Boston, I know the Pauline sisters wear a blue habit. And the Carmelites wear a brown one. Someone should make a reference book of all the habits.

As we walk to the altar, the dome above the nave fills the church with natural light and is surrounded by stained glass windows. It's like being inside a kaleidoscope. I walk around and between people toward what I think is the main attraction: the mosaic above the altar.

The mosaic is the most beautiful I've ever seen. It fills the ceiling and depicts the Sacred Heart of Jesus, with people from all over the world walking toward him. "Each piece of the mosaic is made of glass," Dad says. "But since there are so many of them all placed close together, from afar it looks like a painting."

I can't stop looking at all the details, amazed by the patience of those who built it. I can get tired after just an hour of building puzzles. I'm sure this took much longer than an hour. And how lucky everyone is who gets to stay up praying at night with the beautiful mosaic above them. No wonder Mom came here for Mass when she was studying abroad.

We walk around, looking at the different chapels in the nooks surrounding the nave. There's a chapel dedicated to Saint Joseph, St. Michael the Archangel, and one to doctors. There's also one dedicated to the Jesuits, and to my surprise, there's even one to Saint Ursula. I didn't even know there was a Saint Ursula. All around are stone sculptures. If they weren't attached to the walls, they'd probably be in a museum.

Dad gives me a couple of coins so I can light a candle. It takes me a while to decide where, but I end up picking the chapel all the way back, behind the altar. It's dedicated to the Blessed Virgin. We kneel down to pray for a bit. I thank God for the wonderful trip we're having and ask Mary's intercession for my mom and brother to be okay.

"Ready to go back to the Louvre?" Dad asks after a couple of minutes.

"Definitely," I tell him, reaching out to hold his hand.

18

I THINK ABOUT ASKING DAD IF WE CAN TAKE THE funicular down, since my legs feel a little wobbly from all the climbing. But right before I do, I find Jacques and Monique waiting with a driver from the museum to drive us down the hill and back to the museum. *Phew!*

"We'll come and pick you up in a couple of hours," Monique says as Jacques, Dad, and I get out of the van.

Only a couple of hours? You can't really *see* the Louvre in a couple of hours, not unless you're running through the galleries. But it'll have to do, and I'll have to choose carefully what I want to see.

"I'll be there in a few minutes," Jacques says, putting a piece of gum in his mouth. "I shouldn't chew inside."

Dad and I check in with the guards and walk into the museum. It amazes me how completely different it looks only a few hours later. Tourists really fill up the place. Now there's almost an echo as we walk through the hallways. Personally, I prefer the museum like this. It reminds me of late evenings with Mom and Dad at the MFA.

After walking through a couple of halls, we arrive in front of a staircase. Dad holds me back. "I have a special surprise for you," he says.

I smile and raise my eyebrows.

"But you need to close your eyes," he adds.

"Okay. But if I fall, bump into something, and break it, it's going to be your fault, not mine."

He chuckles, then stops, probably thinking about the not-so-farfetched possibility of me destroying artwork. "We'll be extremely careful."

I close my eyes and then cover them with my hands. Dad holds my shoulders and guides me up the stairs with caution.

"Here's a step . . . and another . . . and another . . . one more."

After what feels like an eternity, we stop.

"Okay," Dad says. "You can open your eyes now."

I lower my hands and open my eyes to discover a statue in front of me. A very *tall* statue. My mouth drops open.

I back up a bit, trying to capture the whole of the statue. I have to go down a few steps to see it without bending backward. *Magnificent* is the word that comes to mind. It appears to be an angel, or so I think because of its wings. I look at the name: LE STATUE DE VICTOIRE. Clearly not victorious, since she's missing her head.

"You know her. That's the Nike of Samothrace, the Greek goddess of victory," Dad explains.

Of course, Nike—or Athena's bestie, as I like to think of her. They led armies together and were believed to be a sort of super-goddess duo, fighting for justice. It was Nike who crowned victors with wreaths of laurel leaves.

"Yikes, poor Nike. She's lost her head," I say.

"I know," Dad says with a huge smile. "I pulled some strings with Dr. Srivas and requested special permission to take a picture of you up there—with your head over the statue."

Behind the statue I can glimpse a movable staircase, similar to the boarding steps used to climb onto small airplanes. A guard is standing next to it. I don't know what to say. I run to Dad and jump up into his arms. He stumbles back a little. I might be a little big for this. Either way, he hugs me tightly.

"As soon as your mom heard I was bringing you on the trip, she asked me to take this picture of you," he says. My eyes tear up a bit. Mom truly knows my heart. "This way, you'll have a picture where your face is on the right direction."

"Thank you, thank you, thank you!" I say. "This is the best surprise ever."

"I'm glad you like it. Why don't you climb up, and we can take the picture?"

It takes me a couple of minutes to put on shoe covers before I'm allowed to climb up the staircase and place my head in a position where it looks natural.

"Raise your head a little higher," Dad says from below.

He'll be taking the picture to make sure it looks great. Following his indications, I stretch my neck up.

"Okay, now a little to the left," he tells me.

I scoot a little to the left.

"Sorry, my left."

He takes about fifteen pictures before he claims to

have the perfect shot. I climb down the stairs carefully, making sure I don't touch anything other than the railing.

"They're amazing!" I tell Dad as he shows me the images on his phone.

"We're definitely printing and framing this one," he agrees.

We continue to walk around the museum. Hall after hall my amazement grows with all the art pieces I get to see. The *Venus de Milo*, the *Mona Lisa*, even some sarcophagi.

Eventually, our time at the Louvre is up. After tonight, Dad is only coming back to the museum to pick up the Regent. The rest of the pieces are being shipped on their own.

As we head out of the museum to meet Jacques and Monique, I hug one of the pillars and whisper, "I'll come back and visit you soon." Although I'd need to visit another country to get another pin on the map, I wouldn't mind making a pit stop in France.

Dad patiently waits for me to finish my goodbyes. I'm grateful Mom and I get to share him.

As soon as we begin walking to the exit, he snaps his fingers and says, "Shoot, I completely forgot to sign some paperwork that Miriam said she'd leave for me. Do you mind coming with me to the lab?"

"Sure," I tell him. Any excuse to spend more time here is a good excuse.

19

IN ORDER TO GET BACK TO THE LAB, A GUARD HAS TO tap his ID badge on a scanner and ride the elevator down with us. When we arrive at the lab floor, he taps his badge again on another scanner. It beeps and allows us through the hallway door.

"I'm going off my shift now," he says. "But someone will be right down to escort you back upstairs."

"Thank you," Dad says. "We don't expect to be down here for long. Should we wait for him in the lab?"

"Oui, s'il vous plaît, yes."

As soon as the elevator door closes again, I rush down the hallway. "Race you!" I call.

"Julieta," he says in a loud whisper, "keep it down.

I know the museum is empty, but you still shouldn't be yelling and running."

Not wanting to get in trouble, I freeze in my tracks. A second later, I feel Dad run past me. *Sneaky.* I can't believe I fell for the oldest trick in the book. I double my effort and run even faster. Dad slows down to let me catch up. That's the least he can do after playing such a trick on me. We round the corner as I take the lead. He speeds up again right before we reach the lab's swinging doors. We arrive at the same time.

"I won!" we both yell and tap the doors.

The doors swing open. To our surprise, there's a man at the back of the room, dressed from head to toe in black. A ski mask covers his face. In his hands he holds a mallet and a chisel.

Those are the only details I notice, because the next thing I know, Dad pushes me out the door and tells me, "Julieta, run and call the guards."

20

I DON'T NEED HIM TO TELL ME TWICE.

I turn on my heels and run back down the hallway. I'm running faster than I've ever run. I glance into each room as I rush through the hallway, searching for a guard. I don't spot anyone. I keep on running.

"Help!" I yell as I run down the hall, desperate for anyone to come to our aid.

No answer.

When I reach the elevator, I slide to a stop. I click the UP button one, two, three . . . ten times before the door opens.

I can't remember what floor the guard's desk is located on, so I click buttons at random until the elevator starts moving. Thankfully, the next floor up doesn't require an ID to access. When the doors open one floor up, I rush out. Another floor full of offices.

"HELP!" I yell once more. "There's a man trying to steal something!"

I don't get an immediate response, so I turn back to the elevator, but the doors are already closed. My heart sinks as I realize I clicked too many buttons, and it will take forever for the elevator to come back.

Desperately I look around for the emergency staircase. I spot a door with a bright neon sign on top that says SORTIE. I run to it and am about to open the door to the stairwell when I see a fire alarm next to it.

Bingo!

This will get everyone's attention. I pull the lever down and wait for people to rush to the hallway. The loud blaring of the alarm brings out a guard only a couple of seconds later.

"Arrêt! Stop!" the guard says, pointing to me.

"Follow me!" I yell back, motioning with my hand.

I don't know if he understands me, but I don't wait around to find out. I open the door to the stairwell and run down, trying to lead him back to the lab. I know the guard is following me because I can hear footsteps behind me. He is also talking fast and in French into his radio.

I arrive back at the lab's floor and find myself locked in the stairwell. I'll need the guard's ID to access the floor. The guard grabs me by the shoulder as soon as he catches up. I try to shrug him off, but his grip is too strong. The fire alarm is still blaring.

"Hey!" I yell, shoving his hand away. "You don't understand. He's going to steal something!"

Panic must be clear in my voice and face, because he drops his hold on me. He speaks into his radio, and after a couple of seconds, a voice comes out. "Yes, I speak English. What is going on?"

The guard places the radio close to my mouth. I need to choose my words closely.

"My dad is Manuel Leal. We're here working — well, not me. He is, my dad. He works for the Museum of Fine Arts in Boston," I say at last. "And he's trying to stop a theft."

By the time the message gets translated back into French, another guard has joined us on the staircase. The three of us rush through the door and down the hall as soon as the ID is swiped on the door. I run full speed through the doors and don't even slow down to open them. Instead I simply extend my arms and ram through like a rhinoceros.

Dad is slumped on the floor. He's not moving. In his hand is a black boot.

21

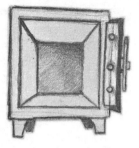

"DAD!" I CRY AND RUSH TO HIM.

When I kneel down next to him and discover he is breathing, I say a silent thank-you to God for keeping him safe. "Dad?" I ask again as I gently tap him on the cheek.

He begins to stir. I try to prop him up, but he is too heavy. The guards that came with me into the room help me sit him up.

Three more guards rush in as we are helping Dad.

"Mademoiselle?" one of them asks. "What happened?" I recognize his voice from the radio.

"Dad and I came into the room, and there was a man all dressed in black . . . " I stop explaining because Dad opens up his eyes.

"Julieta, thank God. Are you okay?" Dad demands.

"Me? Yes. What about you? What happened to the man that was here?" The questions rush out of my mouth.

Dad looks down at his hand holding the boot. He stands up quickly. He wobbles a little and falls back down. The guard catches him just before he hits the floor again.

"Monsieur, sit down, please," the guard tells Dad, pulling him up and pointing to a chair.

Dad waves him off and staggers toward the back of the room, where we saw the man in black standing. Dad reaches the spot and opens the safe's door.

"No, no, no, no," he mutters. "It's gone."

No . . . Is he talking about the . . . ? I walk toward him. When I reach him, he's standing with his arms limp at his sides. The door to the safe box is open, but I can't see inside. I walk behind Dad and peer in from the other side. The only thing inside the safe box is the black velvet square where the diamond was once displayed. The box we packed earlier this morning is missing.

22

THE NEXT FEW MINUTES GO BY IN A FRENZY.

Immediately after we discover that the diamond is missing, a guard speaks rapidly in French into his radio. Another guard calls Dr. Srivas on his cellphone, while another begins questioning Dad and me. They take the boot from Dad's hand. The bright green gum hangs precariously off the heel.

Dad is still a little groggy, so his responses are slow. I'm so in shock I can only give short answers.

"Did you see the man's face?" the guard asks. I shake my head in response. "Did he say anything?" I shake my head again.

The fire alarm stops. I hadn't noticed it was still ringing.

After the guard gets off the phone with Dr. Srivas he announces, "Nobody is to enter or leave the building until the police get here."

We are escorted out of the lab into the hallway so we don't compromise the crime scene any further. A guard brings a chair for Dad to sit in and we wait. He doesn't bring one for me, so I just slump down next to Dad on the floor. We're still there when members of the Paris police force walk in. Some just give us a glance. Another asks us the same questions we've already been asked. A couple of firemen walk down the hallway. (I did pull the fire alarm.)

After about twenty minutes, one of the museum guards walks out of the lab and tells us, "Dr. Srivas is here. Please follow me."

Although nobody states it outwardly, I don't think that the guards trust us, because we happened to be at the crime scene. It feels more like we're being patrolled rather than guided to Dr. Srivas's office — one guard in front of us, two more walking a few steps behind. I glance back a couple of times to see if they're still following us, and each time, one of them looks at me directly in the eyes and frowns.

Do they think we're the ones who stole the diamond?

Miriam's office door is open when we arrive. She's on the phone and pacing quickly from side to side. When she sees us, she motions us all inside.

We stand motionless for a few second while Miriam finishes her call and hangs up.

"Can someone please explain what happened?" she asks the guards. "You call me out of dinner to come back, and the police and the fire department are here."

"Miriam," Dad cuts in before the guards can explain. "Julieta and I were the ones who walked in on the robbery."

"Oh no. What happened?" Her shock makes me think that the guards didn't give her all the details.

Dad quickly tells Dr. Srivas how we had gone into the lab earlier to sign the documents she had left for us, and what we found when we arrived. I explain why it was absolutely necessary for me to pull on the fire alarm so she would know why the fire department is on the premises.

We're interrupted by a knock on the door. Jacques walks in out of breath. He's missing his hat and he's a little sweaty.

"Dr. Srivas," he says, panting. "They need you at

the security office. They're trying to make sure the burglars aren't still inside the museum."

"Julieta, please wait here while we make sure the area is safe," Miriam tells me. "I'll close the door, so please do not open it up for anyone. Okay?"

I nod slowly. I feel like crying a little bit.

"Mr. Leal, please come with me," she tells Dad.

Dad cringes. I wonder if it's because he noticed Miriam called him Mr. Leal, instead of Manuel.

I hug Dad before he walks out. "Be careful," I tell him.

23

MIRIAM CLOSES THE DOOR AS THEY EXIT, AND I FIND myself alone in her silent office. The first thing I notice is that a flag hangs on the back of the door. It's not the French flag. I've seen enough of those in the past couple of days to be able to recognize it immediately: blue, white, and red. The same colors as the US flag, but in three vertical stripes. The flag on the door has three horizontal sections—orange, white, and green. In the middle section there's a blue emblem. There's a blue wheel surrounding a figure that could be described as the product of someone using a Spirograph kit.

I realize my knowledge of flags is extremely limited. *Note to self: study more flags.*

However, I do know some things about Dr. Srivas

that might help me deduce where the flag is from. I walk around the office, searching for more clues.

One of the walls has a large bookshelf filled with books of all shapes and sizes. Most of them have French titles. *L'art contemporain, Art du Moyen Empire égyptien, Art du Monet.* I can't understand some of the words, but they all have the word *art* in them. Contemporary? Egyptian? Monet? I know them. I pull out the *Monet* one, and the cover reminds me of the Impressionism room back at the MFA. I keep looking at the books and discover some have titles in letters I can't even read. The writing is completely different from the alphabet I'm used to. A cluster of bars and squiggles. *It must be fun to write in that language.*

Another wall is full of picture frames. I don't recognize anyone in the photos except Miriam. Underneath the pictures there's a shelf with two small statues standing side by side. One is a bronze statue, which I immediately recognize as a depiction of the Greek god Zeus. A wreath crowns his head. In his hand he holds a lightning bolt, his favorite weapon and most widely recognized symbol. Not many people could hold and wield its power, but he often let his favorite daughter, Athena, use it.

The other statue is wooden. A man sits on an elephant. In one hand he holds the elephant's reins. In two more hands — *Cool! He has four arms.* After looking closely at each of his arms, I discover he also holds two swords and what looks like a rattle. The ends of the rattle look open, like claws, and decorated with a complicated design. Due to the number of extremities on this statue and the fact that it is riding an elephant, I feel confident enough to assume it's a Hindu god. I learned from Geena, the new student at school, that Hinduism is an important religion to many people around the world, especially in India. I wonder which god this is and why he's important.

I really like Geena. She started a week after fourth grade began. I went to her house after school a couple of times, and she showed me all her art supplies. She's the best artist I know! Like Miriam and many women in India, Geena's grandma also wears a sari.

The flag hanging on the door must be an Indian flag. *India* . . . Miriam mentioned India earlier. What did she say about India and the diamond while we were packing today? *The Regent Diamond was actually found in the Kollur Mine in India.*

I'm afraid to continue this train of thought. Could

she have stolen the diamond in order to take it back to its place of origin? Before jumping to conclusions, I want to give Dr. Srivas—Miriam—the benefit of the doubt. She was so nice to me. She let me hold the diamond. But what if she was nice in order to throw everyone off the scent once she stole the diamond? I have no doubt she's smart enough to think ahead and plan something like this.

No, Julieta. Stop making stuff up. You'll get Dad and yourself in even more trouble.

Suddenly, the doorknob rattles and swings open.

24

WHEN DAD FINALLY COMES BACK TO THE OFFICE and opens the door, his hands are covered in black ink.

"Julieta?" He looks around the office, trying to spot me.

"Down here," I answer from under the desk. "I panicked and crawled under it."

"Come on," he says. "Apparently they're gone. The guards and police already checked the museum."

I crawl out from under the desk.

"What's on your fingers? Are we in trouble?" I ask Dad.

"No, sweetie." He hugs me. "It wasn't your fault. We'll catch whoever took the diamond. And the ink is just a precaution. They have to treat everyone initially as a suspect, so they took my fingerprints."

Suspects. I wonder if I should tell him what I found out about Dr. Srivas. I need to make sure, though, before accusing someone. I know Dad doesn't want me starting any more trouble.

"Dad, this flag," I say closing the door and pointing at the flag. "It's the Indian flag, right?"

"Yes. Why do you ask?"

"Well," I begin cautiously, "I was remembering that, earlier today, Miriam—Dr. Srivas—told me the Regent Diamond was actually discovered in a mine in India. A long time ago."

"That's true," he says. "In 1698, a man smuggled it out of the—"

He stops talking the moment he realizes where I'm going with this. He simply shakes his head. "It wasn't her," he tells me. "I know you are a little shaken up by what just happened, but it couldn't have been Miriam. She respects the art too much. Besides, she was at dinner when the robbery happened. And . . . you know how it feels to be accused of something without proof, so why would you do the same?"

She could have been the mastermind and used

dinner as an alibi, but Dad has a point. I felt horrible when Dad thought I had "borrowed" the Athena statuette. But, stealing a diamond from the Louvre seems like a multiple-person job to me. I'm not completely convinced of her innocence, but I don't push the subject, either.

No one says a word on our elevator ride up to the main floor. I walk next to Dad through the museum halls as we make our way to the exit.

"Where are we going?" I ask after a couple of minutes of complete silence.

"For now, back to the hotel," he says. "There isn't much you or I can do right now."

25

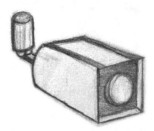

IN THE MORNING I HAVE A HARD TIME WAKING UP.

"Papá, estoy muy cansada," I tell Dad when I open my eyes.

"You kept tossing and turning last night. I think you were having nightmares," Dad explains. "We also skipped dinner last night."

Why on earth would we do that? *Oh, right.* The memories of the previous night rush back.

⚜ ⚜ ⚜

We had skipped dinner last night because I was too exhausted after all the post-robbery mayhem. Dad seemed to age ten years in one conversation, and by the time we left the Louvre, the French police warned us not to attempt any funny business.

"You'll be in town for the foreseeable future, yes?" the detective asked as he caught up to us before we grabbed a taxi. Jacques and Monique had left a couple of hours earlier.

"Until the end of the week, then we fly back to Boston," Dad replied.

"Hmm," the inspector said, looking him up and down. "I wouldn't do that if I were you, not until you have the go-ahead from both the Louvre and my office."

"But my wife—" Dad began. "She's due to have a baby any day now, and I need to get back—"

"Monsieur Leal, you don't want us thinking you're fleeing the country," the inspector said with a hint of a threat. "Your wife will understand. Better to miss the birth of a child than its entire childhood because you're behind bars." With that he turned around and walked back to the Louvre.

By the time we arrived at the hotel, I could only drag myself to bed. Immediately, I was lulled to sleep by Dad's voice, still talking on the phone with the police here in France and the MFA back home.

⚜ ⚜ ⚜

Trying to shake off the memories, I sit up on the bed and rub my eyes. "Dad, did they find the diamond?"

His face droops as he sits down on his bed, and I know the answer before he tells me.

"No, they didn't," he says, massaging his temple. "They're still reviewing the security footage. Some cameras were tampered with, so they're trying to piece different feeds together." He lets out a slow, ragged sigh.

I get out of bed and sit down next to him. "What happens if they don't find it?"

"Well." He takes a moment. "I'm not completely sure yet. I feel like last night I spoke to everyone in law enforcement in France, ending with the *lovely* people from INTERPOL." The way that he says "lovely" lets me know there was nothing lovely about whoever the INTERPOL people happen to be.

"What's that?" I ask.

"It's like the world's police. Countries help each other solve crimes when there is an international component or, in this case, stolen works of art."

"Is there an international jail?" I ask, my voice breaking. Dad hears the worry in my words and hugs me.

I want to cry, but I know it's not the time. Dad must be dealing with so much more, and I don't want to add any more to his already-heavy burden, so I hug him tighter.

"I'm not in that much trouble," he assures me. I sigh incredulously, so he adds, "They know we didn't actually *take* the diamond. There's video footage. However, that doesn't really clear us completely, because they believe we could have been involved. But once we can prove we had no communication with the thief and that we're not working together, we'll be able to go home."

I know *we're* not working together with the thief, but Dr. Srivas pops into my mind once more. However, I still remember my conversation with Dad last night, so I don't say anything else. *I guess I'll have to find some proof on my own.*

26

"WE NEED TO GET GOING," DAD SAYS. "WE STILL have to go to Versailles today to arrange for a chandelier to be shipped. Just because something bad happened doesn't mean life has stopped."

We take quick showers and even quicker breakfasts at a café next to the hotel before Jacques and Monique pick us up and drive us to the outskirts of Paris, toward the Palace of Versailles.

The drive is so quiet that I feel I shouldn't even ask for the radio to be turned on. Jacques keeps glancing back at me. I can only guess he blames me for letting the thief get away.

When we enter the palace, I find comfort and familiarity in discovering my shoes squeak here as well.

Squeak, squeakin', squeak, squeakity.

Jacques takes us to a long, *long* room called the galerie des glaces, or Hall of Mirrors. I've seen pictures of it before, when Dad was showing me the chandelier he'd be bringing down and shipping to the MFA as part of the exhibit. But nothing compares to the real thing. The long room seems to be completely covered in gold. Mirrors along one of the walls reflect the people in the room and make the space seem even bigger and more full of people. Across from the mirrors, the large windows leading out to the gardens let in light that illuminates the entire hall. I look up toward the ceiling. It's filled with paintings.

"I wonder if the painter ever got backaches from painting the ceiling," I say to Jacques, adding a smile to defrost his chilly stare.

Jacques scoffs, turns to me matter-of-factly, and says, "The painter, Charles Le Brun, used to lay down on what you call scaffolds. This way he didn't have to look up while he painted."

I remember laying atop the scaffolding a couple of days earlier. I wonder if being already horizontal allowed Brun to take naps like the one I took. I'm definitely going to try painting like this when I get back home. Perhaps I can construct a scaffold of some sort to paint my room's ceiling. With everything that's happened, thinking about Boston feels like a lifetime ago, instead of only three days.

"The ceiling's beautiful paintings depict some of France's history." His voice reminds me of a teacher's. "In addition, this room is extremely important. The king used to conduct ceremonies in the galerie des glaces. They even had balls here. And these days, the president receives *important* international guests here."

Dad and Jacques walk to the opposite edge of the room into the area supervising the lowering of the chandelier. The area below is blocked off from any tourists. This is the chandelier Dad will be packing up to take back to Boston. I turn to Monique.

"I know how these things go," I tell her. "It's going to take them ages to bring down the chandelier. Let's go explore the gardens."

Monique looks at Dad and Jacques, and a smile appears on her face. "Okay!"

A quick haggle with my dad gets me thirty minutes to explore the gardens. When we walk out to find them, my jaw drops. As far as I can see, and maybe even farther, there are flowers, trees, mazes, and fountains.

I try to imagine the tallest person I know, my uncle Pedro, against the hedges. He could stand on his own shoulders and not reach the top.

"Can we walk through the mazes?" I ask.

"Sure! It's one of my favorite things to do here in Versailles."

I'm glad Monique is so much older than I am. Dad would have never let me go off into the gardens otherwise. I can't wait to be fifteen.

We walk down the palace steps and past a big fountain. "Are those turtles?" I ask, pointing to the figures around its edge.

"On the Bassin de Latone? Yes," Monique says. "The next three levels up have frogs."

We keep walking down the main garden path. As we arrive at the nearest maze, I wonder if we'll receive a map like I usually do in the corn mazes that pop up outside Boston during the fall.

There's no one around to hand me one, so I guess the French must have an excellent sense of direction. I hope for the next best thing, but we don't even get that: a spool of thread like the one Princess Ariadne gave Theseus, the man she loved, when he went into the minotaur's maze.

The half-man, half-bull creature was used as punishment for King Minos's enemies when they were thrown into the unsolvable maze. Theseus wasn't afraid. Instead, he volunteered to kill the minotaur. When Ariadne met with him, she gave Theseus a spool of thread to unravel as he traveled through the maze, which would help him find his way back after vanquishing the beast.

If minotaurs ever existed, they've been extinct for a while now, so I'm not scared to follow Monique as she walks confidently into the hedge structure.

27

SINCE THE SUN HASN'T YET RISEN TO ITS HIGHEST point, the light inside the maze is dim. Walking around, I'm glad Monique seems to know where she is going. I would hate to get lost without an emergency exit like the ones in the corn mazes.

As we walk, Monique and I talk about what we like to do when we're not in school.

"Sometimes I read or help my dad at the museum on busy afternoons," Monique tells me.

"I read too. Still, I wish my dad would let me help out more at the museum." I sigh. "Maybe when I'm older, like you. Mom and Dad only really let me help out around the house—where the objects aren't as valuable as the ones at the museum. Lately, I've been helping Mom a lot. My little brother will be born soon, and she's so big she can't move much anymore."

"I'm an older sister as well," Monique says. "I have a younger brother who is six years old. His name is Martin. My parents also adopted a baby girl. She's two years old now. Her name is Sophie. She used to cry a lot when she was a baby, but now she does many funny things."

"Like what?" I ask, hoping my brother will be funny too.

"Well, she walks very funny when she's trying to kick my football around. Mmm . . . not football. You call it 'soccer'?"

"You play soccer?" My all-time favorite sport.

"Yes, my team finished second last year in the city's junior tournament," she says proudly.

"I also play soccer at my school. I'm a striker, and in our last game I scored three goals!"

"That's really great, Julieta! I'm a goalie. Maybe we'll play sometime." She smiles. "I'll try and stop your goals."

I nod, eager to find some time to play with her. Even though Monique is way older than I am, I'm excited we like a lot of the same things.

After a few more turns in the maze, we walk out into the sun again and are met by another fountain. This one is very wide and has golden horses emerging from the water.

"As you can see," Monique says, "the garden has a lot of fountains."

"The water bill must run high."

Monique laughs. "You're probably right."

This is a subject I know about because Dad hates it when I leave the water running to keep warm when I take a bath.

When we reach the fountain's edge, Monique pulls out a coin from her pocket and hands it to me. "Here. Throw it into the fountain and make a wish."

I stand with my back to the fountain and am just about to make my wish and throw the coin over my head to land behind me, when I hear someone call out, "Salut, Monique!"

Monique and I see Claude walking toward us.

"Bonjour, Claude. How are you?" Monique greets him with a kiss on each cheek. "I want you to meet my friend Julieta. She's from les États Unis."

I give him a small wave with my free hand.

"We've met," he says.

"Yes," I add. "We met at the museum. It's nice to see you again."

"Ah, of course," Monique says. "I guess the theft has me more rattled than I thought."

Claude's face changes at the mention of the theft. He looks like he's gonna throw up.

"Are you okay?" I ask him. "Do you need a barf bag?"

"Me? Oui, oui," he says, wringing his hands. "I need to find your dad, Monique. Is he around? I need to . . . euh . . . talk to him . . . euh . . . give him some papers sent by the museum for him to sign."

"Dans la galerie," she answers, pointing back at the Hall of Mirrors.

"Bon. Then I'll go back to the museum."

"I thought Tuesdays were your day off, since the museum is closed," says Monique.

"Euh . . . yes . . . it is . . . euh . . . they need all the help they can get, so I'm going back."

Monique's face falls, and she begins speaking only in French. I stop paying attention.

While they talk, I can finish my wish. I place my back to the fountain again with the coin in my hand and think about the wish I want to make. I want to pick out my brother's name. *No. Mom is really set on Antonio.* I want to use my coin to help Dad somehow. Yes, that's a good use for a wish.

"I want the thief caught, my dad safe from any trouble, and Antonio to wait for us to be born," I whisper to the coin in my hand.

Hoping the fountain gods don't think I'm cheating for squeezing three wishes into one, I swing my hand as far back over my head as I can and let go of the coin. I know it will go very far, maybe even to the middle of the fountain.

But the coin isn't the only thing that flies off my hands. I realize my bracelet flew off as well when I performed my perfect coin throw. I whip around to see where the coin and the bracelet landed. Thankfully I immediately locate the spot, because great ripples are still on the water's surface.

I can't bear to lose the bracelet Mom gave me along with my new Eiffel Tower charm. People around me might be able to help, but they are all busy taking pictures, or walking around in the sunny day. Monique is still talking with Claude a few yards away. I look back at the fountain and see the ripples are beginning to disappear. If I wait much longer,

I won't know where to find the bracelet.

I have to go in!

Without thinking any more about the matter, I jump into the fountain.

28

A CHILL TRAVELS UP MY SPINE. THE FOUNTAIN IS colder than I'd expected. I take a few steps and regret that I didn't take off my shoes and socks before diving in. My feet get heavier and heavier as I make my way to the center of the fountain.

"Mon Dieu!" I hear a lady cry behind me. Halfway in the fountain I see the ripples are almost gone. A hum grows around the fountain as people begin to notice me. The last ripples disappear as I hear a whistle behind me.

The noise makes me turn, and I see a guard gesturing at me. "Mademoiselle!"

"Just a minute, sir." I make an effort to sound extra polite.

I turn back to the water, the ripples no longer visible. An invisible hand clutches my stomach. I'm standing where the bracelet is supposed to be, but I can't see anything. The waves I created from walking are making the floor of the fountain look blurry, but something glints at the bottom of the pool.

"Claude, help her, aide-la," I hear Monique say.

Preeet! Another whistle behind me.

Ignoring everything, I crouch down and feel around the bottom of the fountain for my bracelet. I touch something and pull it out.

A coin.

I drop it back into the fountain without a second thought. Without a wish. A wasted coin. I plunge my hands in the water again. My splashing is making my clothes wet.

I find another coin.

"JULIETA!" I recognize my dad's voice. Now I'm in trouble. "Get out of there this INSTANT!"

Coin.

"Dad, my bracelet!"

Coin.

"If you do not get out right now . . . "

Suddenly, my hand touches a longer object. It's my

bracelet! I yank it out, and a sharp object scratches the side of my hand.

I stand up and lift it high above my head. "Found it!" I cry as I begin making my way back to the edge of the fountain.

A substantial crowd has gathered around the fountain now. Dad is glowering. Next to him, Jacques is talking rapidly to a guard, who keeps pointing at me. Claude is taking off his shoes before he jumps into the fountain to chase me. *Smart man.* Monique simply stands with limp arms and an open mouth.

I reach the edge as barefoot Claude is just about to climb inside. The guard with the whistle picks me up and out of the fountain. As he sets me down he grazes my hand. I flinch and look down to discover that the scratch is more of a gash and is bleeding.

29

"MADEMOISELLE!" THE GUARD OUTSIDE THE fountain is turning redder by the second. "Il est interdit d'entrer la fontaine!"

I can't understand a word he says. I shrug as a response and hope for the best.

The guard seems frustrated. I can see a vein popping out on his forehead. I've only seen this once before, when I brought a stray dog into our apartment. It had been caught in the rain, and Mom was not happy when she discovered the dog had rubbed itself all over the couch in an attempt to dry itself.

The guard continues screaming at me as someone grabs me by the shoulder and whirls me around.

It's Dad. Jacques stands next to him.

Dad kneels.

Jacques motions to the guard, and they step aside. I assume he begins pleading with the guard for my freedom. As both of them point enthusiastically in my direction, Monique walks up to us.

"What were you thinking?" Dad asks as I press my hand to my stomach to stop the bleeding. People are still gathered around us but seem to be losing interest. Slowly they turn away. Dad's eyes fall on my hand, and his face pales. "Are you hurt?" he asks as he reaches for my hand.

"It's just a scratch," I say, trying to be braver than I feel. The gash, about an inch long, begins to throb.

"I'll ask for a first-aid kit," Monique offers.

Out of the corner of my eye, I see Claude working on getting his shoes back on. Today he's wearing socks that show a boy and a dog. He is wearing a blue sweater and brown pants. The boy, not the dog. The dog is white and has a bone in his mouth. *How many different cartoon socks does he have?*

Jacques is still talking to the guard, who looks less angry now. *Phew*. Hopefully I won't do any jail time.

"Julieta." Dad's voice cracks. "What made you jump in the fountain?"

Is Dad scared? A knot forms in the back of my throat. I show him the bracelet, stained with a couple of drops of blood. Dad looks up from my hand and meets my eyes. He is hurt. I did not behave and got myself into trouble. Unable to hold his stare, I drop my eyes.

"I threw a coin into the fountain, and my bracelet flew off," I explain. "I couldn't bear to lose it."

Dad pulls out a monogrammed handkerchief from his pocket, an anniversary gift from Mom that he cherishes. He wraps it around my hand.

"Manuel," Jacques calls. "They want us to talk to the head guard. They need a statement from her guardian."

I gulp.

30

WITH EACH STEP I TAKE TO THE PALACE, I AM reminded of my crime. My shoes, drenched in water, leave footprints on the ground.

Jacques's phone rings, and he steps aside to answer. He nods at Monique. "Monique, go with them."

Claude hangs back with Jacques. I guess he'll have Jacques sign the paperwork now. Still, I don't see any actual papers in his hand.

There's a breeze I hadn't noticed before. Even though it's a warm summer day, my drenched clothes make me shiver. Thankfully, we soon enter the palace.

Squash, squish, slosh, sloosh.

The once-happy squeaking of my shoes is now

filled with shame. The guard leading us whirls around as soon as he hears the sloshing.

"Ses chaussures," he says to Monique as he points at my shoes.

"Julieta," Monique says, clearing her throat.

I spare her from the embarrassment of having to ask me to take off my drenched shoes and socks. "I know, I know, I know," I say, bending down to untie my laces.

From the corner of my eye, I see Dad turn away from me. He seems to shrink, probably hoping, just like I am, that the earth will swallow us whole. Barefoot in Versailles.

Barefoot in Versailles, I think again. Maybe not even the kings were allowed to do this.

We go farther into the palace. We pass room after room. My feet are now silent on the hardwood floors and rugs. Dad looks straight ahead, not even turning his head to admire the tapestries, rugs, and furniture.

"Dad," I whisper to him.

He doesn't turn around to look at me, but I can still see him clenching his jaw. My head droops. Mom will be disappointed when she hears about this.

We reach the end of an empty hallway. The guard swings open the door and motions us in. The contrast between this room and the rest of the palace is unavoidable. There are metal desks, computers, a coffee machine, and a wall filled with monitors showing the cameras around Versailles. I wonder if my crime has been recorded on one of these cameras.

The guard knocks on a door in the back of the office and opens it. He calls to Dad and Monique and motions them inside the room. I try to follow, but the guard stops me.

"Dad?" I call again. No response.

I slump down on a bench next to the door. It's metal, so another shiver rolls up my spine as my skin touches the cold surface. The office seems to be filled with an eerie silence. A couple of other guards direct curious glances at me, then at the office, then at each other. Unaware of how much they know about my little swim, I simply smile back at them. A couple of them shake their heads.

They know.

I try to make myself as small as possible on this bench. I pull my legs up and hug them with my arms, rest my head on my knees, and close my eyes.

After a minute or so, the guards seem to lose interest, and the hubbub of the office returns. More time passes by, and I jerk up when I recognize Jacques's voice outside the office's entrance. The door to the hallway is ajar, so I peer out, trying to catch a glimpse. He's holding a cell phone against his ear. His voice is agitated.

"That's not the price we agreed on, Sam," Jacques says in English.

I stretch my neck toward the door, hoping to hear more.

"I'll get it done!" His voice is now menacing. "You'll get Athena as long as you keep your promise. I expect to be welcomed with open arms when I arrive in Boston. And no more babysitting jobs. I haven't seen anything special in our visitors to warrant a personal tour guide around Paris. Disastrous is more like it." The word "disastrous" comes out of his mouth as half a growl.

I didn't know he was coming to Boston anytime soon. And Athena? I wonder what the goddess of arts and literature has to do with all of this. Is she part of the exhibit? I thought the exhibit was only about the kings and queens of the world. Yes, her dad was Zeus, king of the Greek gods, so that technically makes her a princess. But it still doesn't make much sense.

The Sam on the phone must have said something that pleased Jacques, because Jacques adds in a much sweeter tone of voice, "And a bigger office than his. I do not want to be stuck in the museum's basement."

Hey! Museum basements aren't so bad. They're like the minotaur's labyrinth, with treasures hidden in its depths. And the MFA's basement is filled with offices. Something clicks in my head. Is Jacques coming to Boston to work at the MFA? There are multiple museums there, but if I recall correctly, Dr. Jenkins's first name is —

31

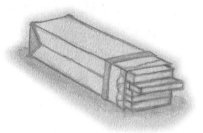

THE HANDLE TURNS AS JACQUES OPENS THE DOOR. Quickly I sit up straight, trying not to move a muscle. Jacques stops short when he spots me.

I smile.

"I'll have to call you back," he says and hangs up without waiting for a response.

"Are you coming to Boston?" I ask.

He ignores the question, clears his throat, and asks, "Where's your dad?"

I point across the room to the office Dad and Monique entered. Jacques looks at the door and then back at me.

"Am I in a lot of trouble?" I ask.

He doesn't answer immediately. Instead, he pulls

out his packet of gum. He removes the silver wrapping slowly. The bright blue stick is enchanting. Bright blue . . .

"For jumping into the fountain? I think I can convince the guards to let you off with a warning," he says.

A sigh of relief escapes me.

"However." He lowers his voice as he adds, "I may not be able to help you if you keep getting mixed up in situations where you don't belong."

I don't think he's talking about the fountain anymore.

"Do you understand?" he asks, putting the piece of gum in his mouth. I'm starting to dislike that bright blue.

I nod.

"Great! Bon, let's get this sorted out," he says and winks at me.

I'm not cold anymore. Still, a chill travels up my spine as Jacques walks into the office.

A couple of minutes later, the office door opens again. The first one out is Monique, who gives me a warm, encouraging smile. Then comes Jacques. He is also smiling, but somehow, I don't have the same feeling of warmth. Dad is the last one to come out, along with a man who I suppose is the head guard. They stop at the door, and Dad turns to shake his hand.

"Merci," he says.

Then Dad turns to me. "Julieta, come here."

I stand up and walk toward them. Maybe if I walk slow, enough time will pass that he'll forget all about the fountain by the time I get there. Unfortunately, I see him tap his feet. He is losing his patience. My slow walking is only making him angrier, so I take giant steps.

"Yes, Dad?" The sweetness in my voice makes me feel empalagada with myself. Just like if I had too much caramel.

"What do we say when we do something wrong?"

"I'm sorry," I say, looking sheepishly at the head guard.

He smiles. "It's okay. Please do not do it again. Otherwise, it's off with your head."

I gasp, surprised.

"Or an equivalent modern-day punishment. Beheading by guillotine is a little frowned upon these days," he adds with a wink.

Phew. I did not want to end up like Marie Antoinette.

32

AT NIGHT, AFTER I TAKE A LONG BATH AND WASH THE fountain off me, I blow-dry my wavy hair. Mom is always saying it's bad to go to bed with wet hair. Before I go cuddle up in bed, I catch a glimpse of myself in the mirror on the wall—I have an animal's mane for hair. Staticky and wild.

Dad, also in his pajamas, sits down on his bed and sighs.

"Dad, can you braid my hair?" I ask him.

He pats the bed, signaling me to sit in front of him. I sit and tilt my head backward so he can reach the hair on top. His hands begin dividing my hair in strands. This isn't the first time Dad has braided my hair. All throughout my kindergarten years, he was the one in charge of getting me ready in the morning. Mom made sure he knew how to expertly French-braid hair like a Mexican teenage girl.

We sit in silence for a few seconds. Then he speaks. "Your mom called while you were having a bath," he begins.

I try to jump up. "Ow!" I cry as I my hair is pulled. For an instant, I forgot Dad was braiding it.

"Sorry," he says, letting go of the braid. "And no," he continues, reading my thoughts. "Not yet. But Antonio will be here soon."

I dramatically slump back down on the bed and add, "Phew!"

In my excitement I undid some of Dad's work. He begins rebraiding patiently.

"I told her about the fountain," he says.

*Uh-oh.*I feel a pang of guilt, remembering I'm supposed to be on this trip to cause less trouble for my parents instead of piling it up on their busy lives. Now that Mom knows about my swim, the promise I made her to help Dad feels even more shattered. "Was she mad?"

"She was a bit upset at first." He puts his hand out so I can see it. "Liga."

I hand him a hair tie I keep handy on my wrist. The same wrist with my bracelet.

"She also laughed," he admits. "But that's not the point. You can't pull stunts like the one today. I know the bracelet is important, but you're old enough to know what is right. You should have called someone."

"I know, Dad," I say. "I panicked."

"I understand that, but you got hurt, and I need to know you can keep yourself safe. You keep asking for more responsibility, like the chance to babysit your brother when he's born, but it's hard to trust you'll do what's right in an emergency."

He pats my back, letting me know my braid is all done. I stand up to look at my braid in the mirror. I'm always pleasantly surprised at how good Dad has become at braiding my hair. He's even better than Mom, even though she had sisters to practice on when she was younger.

Dad adds, "I know it's been just us three for a long time now. However, now that your brother is almost here, Mom and I will begin sharing more responsibilities with you. We'll be especially busy the first year."

"I know, and I do want to do better. I promise," I say.

And I do promise from the bottom of my heart.

"By the way," Dad says, standing up to pull something out of his pocket, "although I don't condone the way you recovered your bracelet, I'm glad you did."

There's a little white pouch resting in the palm of his hand.

"Otherwise," he continues, "where would you hang this?"

I grab the pouch and quickly undo the knot. When I upend it, a tiny silver fleur-de-lis charm falls into my hand.

My eyes tear up, and I hug him. "Thanks, Dad!"

"You're welcome, m'ija," he tells me. "I have to admit I was coming to surprise you at the Versailles gardens. But as we all know, it turns out I was the one surprised with your aquatic display." He chuckles. "I mean, and don't tell your mother I said this, but I'm honestly surprised at the amount of havoc a nine-year-old can cause in less than a week."

I know he's already forgiven me. He's never been the one to enforce punishments. I hand the charm back to Dad, and he helps me attach it to the bracelet. I twirl my bracelet. Now the swan, the Eiffel Tower, and the fleur-de-lis all go on a Ferris wheel ride around my wrist.

"Before you go to bed, please call your mom," he says, handing me the phone.

The video call ring turns my stomach into knots, between missing her and knowing I have probably disappointed her, I can't imagine what our conversation will be like.

33

"Hola, amor," Mom says when her face pops up on my screen. "I heard you went swimming today?"

Phew. If she can joke about it, she can't be that mad. "Sí," I say, and go on to tell her about the rest of my day. After finishing my story, I realize how tired I actually am.

Mom clearly notices and says good-bye. "Nos vemos pronto."

"Yes, I'll see you soon." We hang up.

Dad reaches to turn off the lamp next to my bed.

"Dad?"

"Julieta, we have another long day tomorrow. Please try and get some rest."

"I just have a quick question. It's about something I

heard at Versailles. Did Jacques get a job at the MFA? Is he moving to Boston?" I ask.

"Not that I'm aware. Why?"

I'm not sure I want to tell him how I know.

"Telling Mom about my day reminded me about a conversation I overheard Jacques having on the phone while I was waiting outside the security office," I confess. "He was telling someone something on the phone about Boston, I didn't catch everything. He was on the other side of the door . . ."

Dad puts up a hand, interrupting me. "Julieta," he says, rubbing his temples with two fingers, "please do not eavesdrop on other people's conversations. It's not polite."

"I know, I know," I assure him quickly. "But I thought it would be cool if he did end up working there. Monique could hang out with Robin and me. Did you know Monique is fifteen? So she probably doesn't need a babysitter any more, but still, Robin is pretty cool."

"Why do you think he'll be working there?"

"Well, he was asking for a bigger office at the museum, and he was talking about money—"

"Sweetie,"—Dad cuts me off—"I'm sure you

misunderstood. I think he would have told me if we were going to become coworkers."

"Maybe he doesn't want you to know," I suggest.

"Julieta, first Dr. Srivas and now Jacques? Please do not start conspiracies where there are none," Dad says. "Promise me you'll stop eavesdropping?"

I promise for the second time tonight. However, when Dad turns off the light, I have to admit to myself that this time, my heart isn't truly in it.

34

WE WERE SUPPOSED TO GO SIGHTSEEING TODAY. However, we'll be going back to the Louvre to review the security footage instead.

"They want us to look at it and see if we notice anything else," Dad tells me.

Good. I'm sure the tape will show Dad had nothing to do with the theft. And perhaps it will give the police a clue as to who the real culprit is. I'll also have to be careful about what I say in the room. Dr. Srivas will be there, and if her loyalty isn't one hundred percent behind the Louvre, I can't tip her off about my suspicions.

I make a mental list of the reasons why Dr. Srivas might want the diamond:

- To become rich, duh.
- To wear it, unlikely. It's too big and too obvious.
- To bring it back to India where it was originally found.

Bringing it back to India would be international news. Is that what she wants?

Dad and I get ready and have breakfast by ourselves at the hotel's restaurant. Thankfully, he's in a much better mood today. I remind myself to behave as best as I can and keep the promise I made to him last night.

"Dad, I've checked all the menus and I haven't seen any scarred goats anywhere. Are they only available in special restaurants or is it more of a petting zoo situation?" I ask as we look at the menu.

"The what?" he puts down his menu, confused.

"The scarred goats. Remember? I *think* that's what the flight attendant said I should try."

He starts laughing. "Sweetie, es-car-gots. Not scarred goats. Let's say those are more of an evening meal. And I'm not sure you'll like them even then. They're more of an acquired taste."

"Why? What are escargots?" I ask, trying to copy Dad's pronunciation.

"Snails," he says.

"Eww!" I say a little too loudly.

People at the tables next to us turn around.

Dad starts laughing, and after the initial shock has passed, I join him.

When Jacques and Monique arrive with the van, Dad and I jump in. Nobody wants to talk about the chain of disasters of the past two days. We all spend the first couple of minutes in complete silence. Monique begins tapping her fingers on the window. Then Jacques turns on the radio. The radio host is speaking in French, so I don't understand a word she says.

After another couple of minutes of riding with the radio on, Jacques clears his throat. "So we're having really nice weather, not too hot. Don't you think?"

"Yes, we are," Dad says.

Monique and I just turn to each other and smile.

Another few minutes go by with Jacques and Dad making polite small talk. Forced questions answered with simple yeses and nos. Then only the radio is heard.

I can't take the awkwardness anymore, so I blurt out, "Monique, how many cartoon socks does Claude have?"

"What kind of question is that, Julieta?" Dad turns to me and shakes his head.

Monique chuckles. "Oh, it's fine, Monsieur Leal. He's actually very proud of his sock collection. Did he show his socks to you?"

I can see Dad relaxing in the front seat when he realizes I didn't just put my foot in my mouth. He then begins talking to Jacques again.

"No, he didn't," I tell Monique. "But I caught a glimpse of Asterix at the Louvre, and a boy and a dog at the fountain." I lower my voice at the end. I don't want to remind Dad about my swim yesterday.

"Ah, Tintin," she says. "His comics are quite famous here in France. Tintin is a detective."

I nod, making a mental note to look up Tintin when I'm back home.

"My wife's waiting for us back in Boston, about to deliver our son," Dad is saying in the front seat.

He's talking about Mom.

"It'll be great when you're living in Boston!" I say before I can stop myself.

I immediately know I slipped up, because Dad turns back to me and shoots daggers out of his eyes.

"What do you mean, 'when you're in Boston'?"

Monique asks. She turns to Jacques and excitedly asks, "Are we moving there? Does Mom know?"

"Of course not. She doesn't know because there is no job," Jacques answers.

Next to me, Monique slumps in her seat. "It would be nice," she says in a low voice. "Although I don't know if Mom would let me go and live with Dad."

"Wouldn't you all go with him?" I ask.

"My parents are separated. It's been a couple months, but I think it's going to stay that way. I live with my mom, but during the summer, I try to spend as much time as I can with mon pére, and thankfully the Louvre lets me help out."

"And I definitely would not move unless I had a job already set up," Jacques continues. "Manuel, know about any positions opening soon in the registrar's department?" Then he laughs. It's clearly not a natural laugh, because he clears his throat afterward.

Dad keeps his eyes on me and says, "Not right now, I don't think. I do know they're consolidating some positions together. Making cuts. That sort of stuff." He turns to Jacques and adds, "But you should contact Sam, the curator. He was probably CC'd in some of the emails we exchanged. And if you want, I'll put in a good word for you when I get back."

Sam! Jacques was talking to someone named Sam on the phone. Could it be the same person?

35

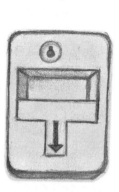

IF IT *IS* THE SAME SAM, WHY WOULD JACQUES DENY having a job at the MFA? Wouldn't it be good news for everyone?

Now I'm presented with a dilemma. On the one hand, I promised Dad I wouldn't meddle anymore, but on the other hand, I should probably let him know that I know who Jacques was talking to on the phone yesterday.

At the Louvre we are escorted directly to the guard's office. For a second I feel like this is what I've been doing the whole trip: visiting security offices of French palaces and museums.

But I don't let this thought distract me from the issue at hand. Right now I'm not the one in trouble, and I need to take advantage of this if I want to find the thief.

"Here," Dad points me to a couple of chairs in front of a humongous monitor. The images on the screen show different galleries in the museum.

Dr. Srivas walks toward us and stands behind our chairs. "Imad," she calls to one of the guards, "please play the clips from the incident."

Images start rolling before my eyes. So far nothing seems out of place.

"If you look closely at these sections," she says, pointing to a couple of screens, "it is clear they have been tampered with. So far that's our theory of how the thief got in without detection."

I look closely at the screen without blinking, trying to figure out how she knows those sections aren't real. After a couple of seconds, I notice a little glitch on the screen.

"Someone recorded a couple of seconds and looped it on top of the real video, and someone else helped from the inside," she explains. "However, we do have some images of the thief. Imad, please pull up the feed from screen seventy-three."

All the other screens disappear, and now we can

only see one that shows an emergency exit. A couple of seconds go by without any changes. Suddenly, a man dressed all in black rushes into the frame and begins pushing the bar on the door to open it. It's locked.

My suspicion about Dr. Srivas being the thief is no longer valid as soon as the thief appears on-screen. The person in the video is way too tall to be Miriam. Back to square one, I guess.

"I have one more screen to show you two," Miriam tells us. "Imad, please include camera forty-five in a split screen."

Another frame pops up on the screen. The hallway is filled with doors, probably offices. I know this hallway! It's where I found the guard by pulling the fire alarm. *Uh-oh.* The video is going to show me pulling the fire alarm. Which you're not supposed to do, unless there is an actual fire.

A couple of seconds later I appear on the screen. I stop for a couple of seconds. The video has no sound, but I know I'm screaming out for help. I run to the end of the hall. The camera switches to a different view and shows me running toward the fire alarm.

As soon as the lights begin flashing, I know what to expect. A guard comes out from one of the offices and begins chasing me. The frame showing the thief is also flashing. The thief stops struggling with the door for a second, looks up at the camera, and smiles through the hole in the ski mask.

"We have certain safety protocols," Miriam explains. "The fire exits are locked. However, once you press the fire alarm, by law and for safety measures, the doors must unlock after fifteen seconds."

I know what comes next. I want to close my eyes, but I need to see what happened exactly. The burglar tries to open the door one more time and succeeds.

It's my fault.

36

I CAN'T BELIEVE I HELPED A THIEF. ASHAMED, I TURN to look at Dad. I want to say I'm sorry, but his face makes me swallow my words. His face is ashen, his mouth is open, and his eyes are wide. He closes his mouth and swallows. His throat must be desert dry, because I can hear it loud and clear.

"I accept all responsibility," Dad says, turning to Miriam. "I told her to go get help, and this was her way of getting help."

"We're not trying to blame anyone except for the one who actually stole the diamond," she replies. "I still have to include this in the full report, and obviously the MFA will receive a copy of it."

"I understand," Dad says.

"This also means you can't leave Paris for a while. Even though Julieta aided the thief in their escape, I don't think they'll hold her in custody. And there's also the question of Odette."

Odette?

Right, the woman who was supposed to bring the cursed diamond to the MFA.

Miriam continues, "She's still missing, so attached to the theft is a missing-person's case."

Dad takes Miriam by her elbow and turns her away from me. I guess he doesn't want me to hear the rest. It doesn't matter, because my head is spinning so fast I can't make out a word they're saying. I can only think about Dad having to stay with me in France and missing Antonio's birth, simply because I got myself in trouble.

I turn to the screen and see the video of the thief looping over and over. The thief opens the door and rushes outside in a wobble because he's missing a shoe. My mind makes the connection to the boot Dad was holding yesterday.

The video loops again.

Such a silly thing, running around with one shoe on and one shoe off. Running around in socks. I focus on the foot missing the shoe. The video loops once more.

"Wait!" I say.

Everyone turns to me.

"Can you freeze that?" I ask Imad. The video stops on a frame right before the thief can no longer be seen on the screen.

"I know who did it!" I exclaim.

37

TOO MANY THOUGHTS ARE GOING THROUGH MY HEAD, and I can't decide what to say first, so I simply point at the foot without a shoe. Both Dad and Miriam move closer to the screen, trying to see what I'm seeing.

"Yes, Julieta," Miriam tells me. "We know about the shoe. There were two sets of fingerprints on them, your dad's and some partial smudged ones. The police are also examining it for any DNA that could point us to the thief."

"No, not the shoe," I say, pointing at the screen. "The sock!" The sock gives me a new suspect. "That's Obelix."

Soon the police are taking my statement of the whole incident once again. This time, I include our encounter with Claude at the museum, his short pants, Asterix, Obelix, and Tintin—which apparently everyone in France is familiar with, because the detectives simply nod when I talk about them. I also tell them about our second meeting at the fountain. They all look a little horrified when I tell them about my jumping in. Then they laugh at me. I get it.

When Dad corroborates my story with what Monique told us about Claude having a great collection of socks, the police begin to take me seriously.

While the guards are still questioning me, Monique and Jacques come into the office.

"I know who's guilty," I tell them as soon as they walk in through the doors.

"You do?" they ask.

I decide to ignore the surprise in their voices and continue, "It was Claude."

Monique is clearly stunned, not sure how to process this information. She reaches around for a chair and slumps down as soon as she finds one.

"I know he's your friend," I tell her. "I'm sorry."

"Julieta." Jacques looks at me without blinking. "What do you mean, it was Claude? Did you see his face?"

His eyebrows are basically touching each other as they come together in a frown.

"No," I begin. Jacques immediately breathes out. "But I saw his sock," I finish.

Jacques's eyes widen. He's clearly surprised I was able to solve this crime faster than the police. "His sock? HIS SOCK! You're blaming him because of his sock?"

Nobody makes a sound. I feel Dad's hand on my shoulder.

"Monique," I plead, "tell them about his socks."

She doesn't move, and no words come out of her mouth.

"Monique," Jacques says, "please go ahead and take Julieta to the hotel. This is no place for her."

I glance up at Dad. He nods, then winks at me. Dad has my back. "Will you take her, Monique?" he asks again, since she hasn't moved.

"Sure," she says, and walks slowly toward me, holding out a hand.

Before taking it, I turn to Dad, but he isn't looking at me anymore. Instead he is staring at Jacques without blinking. I turn to Jacques, only to discover he is also holding the stare with Dad.

"But we haven't had dinner yet," I tell Dad. All the excitement of the day has certainly made me hungry, and I don't plan on missing one of my last meals in France.

"Order room service," he tells me without looking at me. I want to protest again, but something in his voice tells me just to obey.

38

DAD TALKS ON THE PHONE FOR MOST OF THE morning—first with the airline, trying to rearrange the tickets for the next day. Now that the police have another suspect, they are letting us go home. At least for the meantime. He gets two seats for an early flight.

Then Dad calls Mom. "We're not the main suspects anymore," he tells her. "They're investigating Julieta's lead. We're coming home."

Dad then makes other calls. I overhear him telling different people about our trip. The memories from yesterday rush back into my head and make me want to crawl back into bed and stay there forever. Even though I am not directly guilty, I was—how did the police phrase it—*instrumental* in the thief's escape.

I look at Dad's bed. It's still made. Seeing that plus the look on his face tells me he didn't sleep at all last night.

Finally, he gets a call from the police station. His face grows longer with every passing second of the call. He finishes up with a, "Oui, je comprends," and hangs up.

"Did they catch him?" I ask. "Did they arrest Claude?"

"They did."

I jump on the bed, happily hopping up and down and waving my arms. I can't believe I helped catch the thief!

"Julieta, stop that. It wasn't him. They searched his whole apartment and found nothing."

I slump down on the bed. "What do you mean?" I ask. "But he's the one who took it, so he has to have it."

Dad sits on his bed, then changes his mind and stands up again. He paces around for a few moments and finally lies down on his bed. I wait, hoping he'll say it's just a joke, that they actually recovered the Regent Diamond and that we'll go back home tomorrow with it. He doesn't.

"Do we still get to go home?" I ask, afraid of the answer.

"We do." He smiles. "That's the only silver lining. They said they don't have enough to charge Claude, but they don't have enough to charge me, either. I'll have to be in constant communication with INTERPOL once we get back, but otherwise, we're still free to go home tomorrow."

His phone rings again. He looks at the screen, and I'm afraid he's about to cry. "I'll be out in the hallway," he says, kissing my forehead, then walks out the door.

I take a shower, and when I come out, Dad is back in the room, sitting on the bed.

"That was Dr. Jenkins on the phone," he says. "He's also been in contact with the police here." He puts his hands over his eyes.

I sit on the other bed and hug my legs.

His voice is a little muffled when he says, "He said the police already reviewed the street cameras around the Louvre. The thief disappears after a block or so."

Again, he is silent, but I know he wants to say more, so I wait for him to finish. He lies on the bed again, spreads his arms, filling the width of the bed. For the first time I notice that Dad has very long arms. My legs are cramping up a bit, so I swing them around. My feet don't reach all the way down to the floor, but I feel the blood rushing down to my toes.

"We can't actually prove Claude is the one who took the diamond, since we don't have his face on video," he continues after about a minute. "Our best bet was that they'd discover the diamond in his apartment. Since they didn't, the police can't charge him, and he'll be released after twenty-four hours."

"What does this mean?" I ask him.

"It means someone needs to be blamed, and it's going to be me," he says.

So Dad will be the one to go to jail? Technically it should be me they blame. I was the one who pulled the fire alarm, letting the thief escape. Will they send me to jail if I assume the blame?

"Dad," I ask, tears welling up in my eyes, "are you going to jail?"

Dad sits up and looks at me. He sees my eyes, about to burst into tears, and immediately switches beds and sits next to me. His feet do touch the floor.

"No," he tells me. "Of course not. We're still cleared to go home."

Still, I cry.

"I know you're worried," he says. "There was nothing either of us could do. But when you're a grown-up, sometimes you need to take responsibility for things that might not seem fair."

With the back of my hand, I brush away the tears streaming from my eyes. "So what does this mean?"

His voice cracks as he says, "It means . . . they've sent someone else to pick up the art pieces, and . . . I'll no longer have a job once we get back to Boston."

39

"Ladies and gentlemen, welcome to Boston," the flight attendant announces through the intercom as we land. "You may now use your mobile devices, including cell phones. We know you have many different options when you fly, so we appreciate you choosing . . ."

Dad is sleeping next to me, so I lean over him to open the window shade. He stirs, and like every other passenger, turns on his phone as soon as he opens his eyes. I don't own a cell phone yet, so I take this time to look around the cabin. A man a couple of rows in front of us has two phones and a tablet out. The woman sitting across the aisle from me is frantically attempting to pull out her bag from under the seat in front of her.

Next to me, Dad gasps. "¡Dios mío! I have eleven voice mails from your mother."

"Is she okay?" I feel a knot forming in my stomach. Mom is not the kind of person to leave voice mails. She says if she wanted to talk to a machine, she would talk to her kitchen appliances. The eleven voice mails mean she was desperate to reach Dad.

"I don't know yet." Dad's brow is furrowed as he begins listening to the messages. He takes a deep breath and doesn't let it out until he tells me, "She started having contractions."

I don't know much about labor, but I do know contractions are an important part of it. That means Mom is in the process of giving birth to my baby brother. I remember her practicing her breathing on the living room couch and telling me it would be useful to keep her calm and sane once the contractions came.

"Is she at the hospital already?" I ask.

"I don't know," he says. He selects the next message in the queue.

After a couple of seconds, his brow relaxes, but his eyes widen. He shoots out of his seat. Unfortunately, he was sitting in the window seat, so he bumps his head on the overhead compartment. The people in the seats in front of us turn around to look at him.

"Ow," he cries. "Julieta, grab your things. We need to get off this airplane immediately. Your mom is on her way to the hospital."

More and more people are turning around in their seats to look at the man causing a commotion in the cabin. A flight attendant walks our way. *Uh-oh. He's in trouble.*

"Come on, Julieta, quickly!" Dad urges.

I'd rather be in trouble with the flight attendant than with Dad, so I lift the tab on my seat belt and release it. I bend down and begin fumbling around, trying to get my backpack out from the seat in front of me. My hands are shaking a little bit. *I'm about to be a big sister.*

"Come on, Julieta," he says, urging me again to stand up.

"Dad, I can't reach my backpack."

He presses another button, moving on to the next voice mail. His eyes widen more — if that's even possible.

"Sir." The flight attendant has reached us. "You need to sit down while the plane is moving."

Without paying any attention to her, he says to

me, "They already admitted her in the hospital. She's having the baby."

People are now blatantly staring at us. The commotion around us is growing. I think they're trying to guess what's going on.

"I want to listen," I plead.

He puts the phone on speaker.

"Sir," the flight attendant says, "I'm going to have to ask you one more time—"

Mom's voice interrupts her. "Manuel, honey, I love you, and I know you want to be here, but Antonio doesn't seem to want to wait any longer." Her voice is strained. "Call me as soon as you land."

Dad slumps back into his seat. He clicks on the next voice mail.

"Where are you?" Mom's loud grunts come out of the speaker for everyone to hear. "He's not waiting any longer. This kid is coming out right now."

There're a couple of seconds of silence from the phone. And the cabin. Everyone is paying attention to Mom's voice message.

We hear someone in the background. "Okay, Erica, time to push again."

The message ends right there.

I can feel Dad shaking a little bit, so I hold his hand as he selects the next message.

"Manuel." Mom's voice is tired but relieved. "I can now proudly say that you have a beautiful son."

Dad and I look at each other. An eerie silence surrounds us. I realize everyone is looking at us, waiting for our reaction. Even the plane stops for a second on the tarmac.

"I have a son," Dad whispers quietly to himself.

I stand up on my chair and announce to the whole plane, *"I'm a big sister!"*

The plane erupts in a cheer. Shouts of congratulations reach my ears.

"Sir, congratulations and all, but we really need both of you to sit back down and put on your seat belts," the flight attendant tells us.

Everyone is still clapping when we arrive at the gate

40

UNABLE TO REACH MOM AFTER WE GET OFF THE PLANE, we listen to the other five messages she left for Dad after we get through customs, once we get in a cab:

1. "Manuel, he has your eyebrows." *Beep*.

2. "Thankfully he has my ears." *Beep*.

3. "Also, we're all good on the extremities front. Ten fingers, ten toes." *Beep*.

4. "Julieta, you're gonna love his sneezes. You just missed one. It was the cutest thing ever." *Beep*.

5. "He just opened his eyes. Wait, he's closing them again. Ah, he's opening them up again." *Beep*.

We sit in the backseat of the cab speechless for about ten minutes before Dad breaks the spell. "I should call Robin."

"Robin? Is she with Mom? Wait . . . No! Please don't!" He's planning on taking me home. "I don't need a babysitter!"

"I'll drop you off at home," he tells me. "You can meet your baby brother tomorrow morning."

"Do I have to? It's not even my bedtime. The sun is still up." I hope he'll change his mind.

"Yes, you have to. The sun might still be out, but you're on Paris time, and it's much later there. Besides, I want to talk to your mom about the most recent developments of our trip."

I know he's still hurt about losing his job, but he shouldn't take it out on a new big sister. I turn to the window and refuse to speak to him. The city lights grow larger as we cross the Harvard bridge on our way home.

41

I MUST HAVE FALLEN ASLEEP IN THE CAB, BECAUSE I wake up in my bed, not really knowing how I got here. I walk to the kitchen, hoping to see Dad. The only person in the room is Robin.

"Hi!" she greets me with a smile. "I heard you became a big sister last night."

I'm still half asleep and extremely tired from the trip, so I grunt as a reply.

"What do you want for breakfast? I can make some eggs if you want."

"Eggs are fine," I tell her in a croaky voice. I clear my throat and ask, "Where's Dad?"

Answering my question, Dad opens the apartment door. "Good morning, sleepyhead." He kisses the top of my head. "You'd better be ready soon so I can take you to meet your brother."

Forgetting all about my eggs, I run to the bathroom to take a shower.

"You still need to have breakfast," I hear Robin call from the kitchen.

"I'll take it to go," I say, poking my head out the bathroom door.

When we finally reach the hospital, I discover its policy discourages visitors under the age of twelve. However, I am relieved to find out that siblings of all ages may visit newborn babies.

Since I'm a big sister now, I stroll in like I own the place. Under my arm I carry a box that holds Antonio's gift from France.

"We're here!" I announce when I walk into the room.

Mom is lying on the bed with her back to us. "Julieta, corazón," she whispers as she turns. She's wearing a hospital gown but has a big smile on her face. She places her index finger on her lips, signaling me to be quieter. "Your baby brother is asleep."

She opens her arms wide, inviting me to hug her.

I turn to hand the gift to my dad. Before I run to Mom, I ask him, "May I?"

He gives me a smile. "Slowly."

I nod and walk toward the bed at what feels like a turtle's pace, but I know I need to be careful.

"Please walk faster," Mom says. "I've missed you so much."

I speed up and climb onto the bed. "Hi, Mom," I say, and give her a careful hug.

She squeezes. I squeeze back a little.

I feel Dad's arms around me as he hugs us both. "Family hug," he says.

It feels like it's been forever since we were all together. The trip seems like it went by so fast, but at the same time, it took too long. The warmth of being surrounded by my parents makes me grateful to be their daughter. Which makes me remember . . .

"Wait!" I say. "We're forgetting Antonio. Where is he?"

Turning around, I discover there is a small crib on the other side of the bed. "Is that him?" I ask Mom.

She nods and turns to Dad. Dad's eyes are glistening. He kisses Mom on the lips.

My vision blurs, I'm so happy. I love my family. I

love being a big sister. *I'm a big sister.*

I scoot closer to look at his tiny nose and tiny lips. "Can I touch him?"

"You can even hold him," Mom says to my disbelief. "Just wash your hands first."

I rush to a sink in the corner of the room and wash my hands. At school I learned you're supposed to sing the happy birthday song twice to make sure you've washed your hands long enough. *Happy birthday to you. Happy birthday to you —*

I stop midsong. *Funny, yesterday actually was Antonio's birthday.*

I decide to sing out loud the second time around.

Mom and Dad are laughing when I come out of the bathroom. "What was that?" Mom asks.

"Well," I explain, "yesterday *was* Antonio's birthday. So I thought it appropriate to sing the song. Unless the nurses sang for him. Then I'm a day late."

"Take a seat in the armchair," Dad says, already holding Antonio.

Flying to the armchair wouldn't have gotten me there fast enough. When I sit down, I begin to feel nervous. What if I drop him? What if he doesn't like me? What if I'm not a good big sister?

I think Mom notices this, because she says, "Julieta, hold your arms like this."

She forms a circle with her arms and then pulls them closer to her. I nod and copy her movements.

"Ready?" Dad asks.

I feel ready, so I nod once more.

"Careful with his head. He's not strong enough yet to hold it up."

I turn my hand so it cradles his head. Dad places Antonio carefully into my arms. He's heavier than I had expected, but I can still hold him. He smells new. But not like a new toy. Like a new baby. Immediately I know I love him. That I'll teach him everything I know and protect him.

I try to hug him a little closer, but he shifts a little in his blanket. I freeze. Daring not to move an inch, or even breathe, I turn my eyes to Dad.

"It's okay," Dad assures me.

I let out my breath slowly.

Antonio opens his eyes.

"Hi, Antonio. Soy tu hermana, Julieta."

He blinks a couple of times. Then he stares at me.

I don't know what else to say, so I begin singing "Buenos Días Señor Sol."

He doesn't cry, so I guess like Mom, Antonio also loves Juan Gabriel. I smile, thinking about how Antonio will grow up like me, listening to old Spanish and English songs. I look up at Dad to point this out and I see him recording us on his cellphone. I stop, feeling a little shy.

"He's so lucky to have you for a big sister," Dad says. "I know you'll help take care of him."

I kiss my brother on his little forehead. *I definitely will,* I think, making one more silent promise.

42

BEFORE GOING HOME, WE STOP AT THE MFA.

"We might as well get it over with," Dad says.

His shoulders are drooping as we walk up the steps to the museum. I hold his hand, and he gives me a little squeeze. When we were at the hospital, Dad told Mom that if he doesn't get another job soon, he could take care of Antonio while she works. This made me think he wasn't terribly sad about it, but now his drooping shoulders tell another story. I think he's going to miss walking the halls of the museum every day and taking amazing trips around the world making sure the artwork is safely packed and shipped.

Inside the hallway with the offices, he tells me,

"Julieta, I need to go clean out my office." His voice cracks. "Please go ask Joanna if she can help you find some empty cardboard boxes."

"Sure, Dad." I squeeze his hand once more and let go.

Joanna used to let me help out at the museum. I don't think I'll be allowed "backstage" anymore. I'm pretty sure I'll be banned from the museum—and all museums—for all eternity. Even if I came with Mom, it might be good for the MFA and me to put some distance between us. At least for a while.

"Hi, Joanna," I say as I walk into the office.

"Julieta!" She gets up from her desk and hugs me. "It's great to see you. Did you enjoy your trip to Paris?" She immediately covers her mouth with her hand. "I mean, I know it didn't end well. But hopefully you still had some fun?"

"Yes," I tell her, thinking back on the trip. "The Eiffel Tower was my favorite part. I got this charm there." I lift my hand to show her.

"Oooh, that's pretty," she says. "I remember my first time in Paris. It was more wonderful than I could have—"

Behind us someone clears their throat. "Hi. I'm looking for my father."

I turn to discover Monique standing in the doorway. What is she doing here?

43

"You must be Monique," Joanna says, shaking her hand. "Your father just went into a meeting with Dr. Jenkins. You can sit down and wait for him if you like."

"Thank you," she says and walks to the sofa in the room.

"What are *you* doing here?" I ask — in an accusatory tone, if I'm being honest.

"Dad brought me along to help with the collection." She hesitates. "I mean, the museum asked for someone to accompany the rest of the exhibit to Boston."

I shrug. I know it's not Monique's fault Dad was fired. But somehow it still doesn't seem fair. Dad didn't do anything wrong, either, yet he is packing up his things right now. Which reminds me . . .

"Joanna,"—I turn to her—"my dad needs some empty cardboard boxes to pack his office. Could I grab some?"

Joanna smiles. "Sure thing. I'll ask Jerry to bring some." She looks at the radio and turns back to me. "Or do you want to radio him?"

It would be a little too painful to use my last radio call to help kick out Dad. "Nah," I tell her. "I'm good."

"Of course." She radios Jerry.

Five minutes later I walk into Dad's office with four unfolded cardboard boxes and the news that Monique and Jacques are here. However, before I tell Dad I stop short and absorb the view. About two hundred books are all over the floor.

He claps when he sees me. "Great! You can begin with these stacks of books," he says, pointing to the stacks closest to the door.

We finish packing after thirty minutes and two more trips to the main office for boxes. Most of the contents of his small office were books.

"Dad," I say with my hands on my hips, "soon it will be either us or the books in our apartment."

"Yeah," he says, scratching his head. "So which friend's house will you be living in? I mean, I still would like to see you from time to time."

I squint at him. *He's joking . . . right?*

His lips quiver, trying to hide a smile. A sigh of relief escapes me. "Mom would kick *you* out first," I tell him.

He smiles. "You're probably right," he says, playing with my hair. He leans over to pick up a box. Grunting, he straightens up again. "I don't think we can take all of these today. We still need to build the crib and figure out where to fit everything."

"We could use a dolly to carry them home," I suggest. I love using the dolly.

"That's crazy talk," he says. "Let's ask Joanna if they can hold them for a bit while we organize everything back at home."

We walk back into the main office, Dad carrying a box, me holding his briefcase. Monique, still sitting on the couch, is now reading a book. I tilt my head to try and read the title on the spine, but I'm interrupted by the *thump* of Dad setting down the heavy box he was carrying on Joanna's desk.

"Joanna," he says, "I need a favor."

"What's up?" Joanna asks, looking up from behind the box.

"Do you think you could store my stuff for a while?"

"How much time are we talking about?"

I know Joanna would love to help Dad if she could, so I'm a little surprised by the question. Apparently, so is Dad, because he hesitates a little before continuing.

"Uh, just a couple of days," he says. "Just until I can make some space for them at home."

"Oh," Joanna says. "Sure. That's okay! Sorry about that. We'll be moving around some of the offices to make space for Dr. Legrand, but I don't think that will happen for another week."

What? He's getting an office?

"Sure . . . sure," Dad says absentmindedly. "Wait . . . who did you say is getting an office?"

"Dr. Legrand from France. You did meet him there, didn't you?" Joanna asks, confusion showing on her face.

"Yes, we did," Dad admits. "I just didn't know he was working here."

"It was a last-minute arrangement," Monique says

behind us. "I think we basically got on the next plane after you left."

Dad turns, surprised. Clearly, he hadn't been aware of her presence. "Monique. I hadn't noticed you there."

"Hi, Monsieur Leal," she says sheepishly. "I'm glad to see you again so soon."

"Yes," Dad says disconcertedly. "It's great to see you too. Your dad is here?"

She points at Dr. Jenkins's closed door.

"Ah," Dad says. "Of course."

The four of us stand there in silence. We look at one another. Nobody wants to be the first one to talk.

"So, Monique," I venture, "you should visit the Freedom Trail when you get the chance. You can walk all around downtown Boston, learning about the American Revolution."

That seems to break the spell, because Dad turns to Joanna and asks, "You need me to sign something before I leave?"

"Right!" Joanna says, shuffling some papers on her desk. She hands Dad two sheets and points to the bottom of each. "Here and here."

Dad grabs a pen from the desk and begins signing.

Before he finishes, the door to Dr. Jenkins's office opens, and both Dr. Jenkins and Jacques walk out.

"Manuel," Jacques says in surprise, "I didn't know you were going to be here. I thought you'd be with your wife. Dr. Jenkins told me congratulations are in order?"

Jacques stretches his hand out. Dad reluctantly shakes it. I turn to see Dr. Jenkins eyeing me.

"Yes, we actually came from the hospital," Dad explains. "I just wanted to get the packing in my office done."

Dr. Jenkins is still looking at me when Dad tells him, "I'll be back for the rest of the boxes in a couple of days. I already set that up with Joanna, sir."

"Yes, that's fine," Dr. Jenkins answers.

At that moment, something red behind Dr. Jenkins catches my eye. I tilt my head around him to see what it is. A red ribbon on a bust. *Funny*. It looks almost as if the ribbon was a shiny tie around the head of . . .

44

"Is that a bust of Zeus?" I ask, pointing inside his office.

"Ah, yes," Dr. Jenkins says. He turns around quickly and shuts the door to his office. "A little present from Jacques. When we talked on the phone yesterday, I mentioned I was a fan of the *Jupiter of Smyrna* they have at the Louvre, so he got me a life-size bust from the museum's gift shop."

Wait. Zeus was called Jupiter by the Romans.

Jupiter . . . *Zeus*.

Zeus . . . Athena.

Of course! I feel fireworks go off in my head. Jacques's phone call with Sam.

"That's a nice gift," Dad says. "We should be getting back home, Julieta."

"Zeus, King of the Gods." I wave my hands in front of me, drawing an imaginary marquee in the air.

Joanna chuckles.

"Fit to be part of the exhibit," I say.

Jacques smirks. "You really do know your mythology, Julieta."

"I do. Greek mythology is my favorite," I say. "Although I would have preferred another god as a gift."

I have everyone's attention now.

"Don't get me wrong," I explain. "Zeus is interesting and everything. But Athena . . . I've got a special place in my heart for Athena."

And there it is. A tiny twitch on Jacques's face that I wouldn't have seen if I hadn't been looking for it.

"Come on, Julieta," Dad says. His voice seems a little dry. He's clearly uncomfortable in this situation.

Almost everyone seems to be. Joanna and Monique look around, seeing everything and nothing. Dr. Jenkins taps his fingers against his side.

Only Jacques and I seem to be invested in the moment. We both look at each other, measuring each other, refusing to give an inch before the other one does.

"Julieta, we should get back home and set up the crib," Dad says. "Your mother is coming home from the hospital tomorrow."

"Yes, and I have much work to do," Dr. Jenkins says, turning around and opening his door.

Bingo! Here's my chance.

I spring past him before anyone can blink.

Anyone except Jacques. "Stop!" he yells, trying to grab me before I enter the office.

I dodge him, slapping his arm out of reach. I run to the desk where Zeus's head stands. Royal and fierce. Not for long.

I grab the bust and hold it over my head. It's heavier than I thought it would be.

Before I can do anything else, Dad yells, "Julieta! Stop this instant!"

I freeze out of habit. Dad's furious voice always makes me stop in my tracks. Apparently, it works on other people too, because nobody moves. Not Jacques, not Dr. Jenkins. Joanna and Monique are peeking behind everyone else, but they don't dare move, either.

"Dad," I say, "if Antonio were a girl, I would vote for the name Athena. Did you know she was born from Zeus's forehead?"

"What does that have to do with — ?"

Before he finishes the sentence, I slam the bust as hard as I can against the floor. The bust breaks into hundreds — no, thousands of pieces. Dad, Monique, and Joanna look at me like I've gone crazy. Jacques and Dr. Jenkins pale. On the floor, in the middle of the room, surrounded by the bits and pieces of what used to be the mighty Zeus, is a little black pouch. I immediately pick it up before Jacques and Dr. Jenkins recover from the shock.

"Dad," I say, offering up the pouch.

Without me having to say anything more, he knows what's inside. "Joanna, call security immediately," Dad says.

He doesn't need to tell her twice.

45

THE REST OF THE DAY GOES BY IN A FLASH. THIS TIME, I'm actually glad to be in a police station. For the first time in my life, I'm on the right side of the law and questioning the suspect. Well, okay, questioning might be an exaggeration.

After I discovered the diamond, security was called. Then the police were called. Chaos ensued, the museum was shut down for the rest of the afternoon, and news anchors showed up outside the museum entrance, trying to interview anyone who knew anything. Dad didn't let me talk to anyone. At least not until everything was cleared up with the police.

To help the investigation go more quickly, I stand on the other side of a one-way mirror with Detective

Charles from the Boston Police Department, watching the questioning happening in the next room. It's just like the movies! We can see them as if looking through a window, but they can only see a mirror. The Boston police, who are working with INTERPOL, want me to listen in and fact-check Dad's version of our trip and the robbery. Dad goes first. He knows less than I do, so every now and then I have to fill in the blanks.

"Well, I guess Julieta knew somehow that *Athena* was the code name for the diamond," I hear Dad say through the intercom.

Detective Charles stands next to me and gives me a sidelong look. He's barely said a word since I walked into the room, but after a couple of side glances, I know what he's expecting.

"Actually," I explain, "I eavesdropped on a phone conversation between Jacques and a person called Sam, who I'm positive now is Dr. Jenkins—"

I stop, because it's still hard to believe he was involved in any of this. The man who provided me with so much candy turned out to be a bad guy. Unfortunate. Hopefully, whoever they choose as the new museum director will keep a candy stash—and steal less. I guess that's more important.

Detective Charles clears his throat and looks at me. His deadpan eyes tell me he wants me to elaborate.

"He mentioned the name Athena," I continue, "and I do love Athena. Athens, the city, is actually named after her, the goddess of wisdom."

Detective Charles looks up from his pad. "I did not know that."

"Anyway, he mentioned Athena in the phone call, saying he'd get Athena to this Sam. I was a little confused, since I wasn't completely sure if he was speaking to Dr. Jenkins, and which Athena they were talking about. But then, when I saw Zeus's bust, it all made sense."

I cross my arms, satisfied with my deductions.

"I'm afraid you lost me there," he tells me. "I thought we were talking about Athena."

"Ah, yes. Athena was Zeus' daughter. She was born from his forehead. That's why she's so smart. The bust was a depiction of Zeus. So I put two and two together and got four. Four . . . forehead."

"Mm-hmm." Detective Charles seems amused with my play on words. "This is quite helpful," he tells me as he continues to furiously scribble on the little pad. "We'll check the call logs on both their phone accounts from the day you mentioned and use it as evidence."

After some more questioning, Dad is led out of the examination room by a police officer. I make a move to leave, but Detective Charles stops me. He points to the door in the room behind the glass, and I see Jacques brought in. The first thing I notice is he's in handcuffs. This is the first time I've ever seen a handcuffed person in real life. All my previous experiences have been through the television screen.

Detective Charles turns to me. "He has already admitted guilt. Smart for a man who was basically caught red-handed. Unlike Dr. Jenkins, who refuses to admit he did anything wrong, I'm sure Jacques's sentence will be lessened once he begins cooperating. However, I'd like for you to come back after lunch and listen to his testimony, help connect any missing links. We want to make sure we have all the evidence. Do you think you're up for it?"

"Absolutely," I answer.

46

AFTER LUNCH, I FIND MYSELF BACK AT THE STATION AND next to Detective Charles. I don't want to admit that I feel a little nervous, so to hide it, I try my best to remain still. The energy surging through me, though, makes it impossible, so I allow my hands to fidget behind my back.

On the other side of the one-way mirror, Jacques begins talking to a police officer. After a few minutes, I realize there was a lot I didn't know about.

"Claude was the one who actually performed the robbery," Jacques tells the officer. "He was in it mostly for the money, although I did promise to bring him on my team after I had been working at the MFA for a couple of years. That made him really eager to help Sam and me out."

"Claude. Yes, apparently we have him on tape with what seems to be"—the officer reads in his notes—"an Obelix sock on?" He turns to the one-way glass, clearly confused.

"Yes, from *Asterix and Obelix*." I nod at Detective Charles. "It's a popular comic in France."

Once again he waits for me to elaborate on my vague answer.

"Claude is a fan of what I call some peculiar socks. The morning we met at the Louvre, I noticed he was wearing an Asterix sock. I didn't see Obelix, but I assumed it would be a pair."

"Mm-hmm," Detective Charles says, scribbling some more.

We both turn back to the examination room.

"How did he get into the museum? There is no record of Claude swiping his card that night," says the officer.

Jacques scoffs. "Well, it was obviously my ID that was used."

"Obviously!" I say.

"Is it?" Detective Charles asks.

"Yes," I say. "He stayed back to chew gum and probably spat it out before they both walked into the museum. Gum is very sticky. You know, I haven't had gum in a very long time because last time I did, I blew a bubble so big it popped all over my face, and long story short, I was missing a chunk of hair for a couple of months until it grew out."

"Still not seeing the obvious."

"I thought you had received the police report," I say. "There was a piece of gum stuck on the boot. Blue gum. Bright blue gum. The same gum Jacques chews to stop smoking."

"Nasty habit," Detective Charles says, nodding.

"And what role did your daughter, Monique, play in the robbery?" the officer asks Jacques.

He lowers his head. "I already told this to the other officer: absolutely none. She's completely innocent and knew nothing about what Dr. Jenkins, Claude, and I planned. It was an unfortunate coincidence that she met Claude and introduced him to me. She thought she was helping him find a career working in museums."

"Ask him what happened to Odette," I tell Detective Charles.

"Who's Odette?" he asks me.

"I'm not really sure." I shrug. "She was supposed to bring the diamond to the MFA. She was the original handler. But she's missing, and that's why Dad was in charge of the diamond."

Detective Charles presses a button on the intercom and asks, "Where's Odette?"

Jacques looks up at the one-way mirror and laughs, surprised. "I needed to shift the security protocol for the robbery, so I told her she was off for the next couple of weeks. Gave her fake paperwork giving her time off and everything. I guess she went camping?"

Detective Charles looks at me for confirmation. "I know nothing about that," I say. He responds by scribbling furiously on his notepad.

"And how did you smuggle the diamond out of France and into the US?" the officer continues in the other room.

"In my briefcase," Jacques admits. "You see, diamonds don't light up in airport x-rays, at least not like liquids or metals. So if you don't know what to look for, it will be hard to see diamonds. It was also covered by the plaster in the bust, which I had a receipt for from the gift shop and showed to the officer."

"Okay," Detective Charles says, standing up. "I think we're done for now."

As he leads me out of the room, I look back and

catch a glimpse of Jacques through the one-way glass. He rests his head on his handcuffed hands.

Dad is waiting for me in the station's lobby. "Thank you, Julieta, for helping the detective," he says, hugging me.

"I tried my very best," I say, not letting him break the hug yet.

As Dad and I walk out of the police station, we bump into Monique outside talking on her cellphone. I can tell she's been crying when she turns to look at us, because her eyes are puffy and red, which makes them look greener than usual.

"Monsieur Leal, Julieta," she begins, "I want to apologize on behalf of my dad —"

Dad waves her off with a hand. "Monique, sometimes it's important to take responsibility for the actions of others, but not in this case. None of this is your fault, so please don't apologize. I'm just sad you had to experience all of this."

"I agree with Dad. What will you do now?" I ask, wondering if she'll be staying or going back to Paris.

"Joanna, the woman from the museum, helped my mom to arrange a hotel room for me tonight. Tomorrow I'll be going back home to France," she says, sighing.

"I begged Maman to let me live here with my father for the first semester, and she was planning on sending my clothes here next week." She lets a breath out. "I guess that's not going to happen anymore."

"I guess not. But hey," I tell her, "you can come visit us any time you like. I'll take you on a tour of the Freedom Trail, and you can help me babysit Antonio. He's the cutest baby. Dad, can I borrow your phone to show Monique pictures of the baby?"

I'm happy to see a smile on Monique's face once I start showing her all the pictures Dad took. Dad nods at me and Monique. A sigh of relief escapes me.

47

THE NEXT MORNING I WALK INTO THE KITCHEN, EX-pecting to see Robin there again. Instead, Dad is making breakfast.

"Your mom isn't being released until later today, so I thought we could have breakfast together. I prepared escargots, since you didn't get a chance to try them in France."

"No, gracias. No me gustan los caracoles," I tell him with a smile.

"Fine," he says with a wink and opens the fridge. "How about blueberry pancakes, then?"

I give him a giant smile. Blueberry pancakes are Dad's specialty. That, and chilaquiles verdes.

"I have some news," he says, placing the first

blueberry pancake on my plate.

I take a huge bite. "What news?" I ask with my mouth full.

"They found Odette," he says. "Funnily enough, she was camping, out of phone reception, and didn't even know what happened until she came back to a full voice mailbox and police officers waiting at her apartment."

"That must have been scary," I offer, taking another bite.

"Definitely," Dad says. "But that's not all. Thanks to yesterday's events, the museum's board of trustees convened an emergency meeting last night. In the search for a replacement museum director, a name you might recognize came up as an option."

I stop chewing, waiting for him to tell me the name.

"They're considering bringing Dr. Srivas from the Louvre."

Miriam!

"That would be an amazing choice," I tell him with my mouth still full of blueberry pancakes. "She'll be able to see her daughter all the time. Tell the board they have my absolute approval."

Dad chuckles. "Okay, I'll let them know how you feel."

I take another bite.

"There's more," he tells me. "After we left the station yesterday, I got a phone call from Miriam. She told me she was grateful for all you did for the museum and that she had overnighted a gift for you, all the way from the Louvre. A special messenger dropped it off this morning."

He hands me an envelope. I can feel something hard at the bottom, so I open it and reach all the way down inside. My hands wrap around yet another pouch. I pull it out and open it up. Inside is another charm.

I show Dad. "The Louvre Pyramid. It's beautiful."

"I'll call Miriam," Dad tells me. "That way you can thank her personally . . . and best not mention you ever thought she was the thief. No need to make her feel bad about something she never knew."

My stomach drops. Looking back on the past week, I can't believe I ever thought Miriam would ever be a part of a diamond theft.

"I'm sorry about that, Dad. I should have treated her the way I want people to treat me. Especially around art."

Dad nods. "I think finding the diamond clears your art-wrecking slate." He hands me his phone.

Miriam's contact information is already on the screen. "Whenever you're ready."

Without wanting to make it harder, I press CALL.

Miriam's voice comes on the speaker. "Hello, Manuel?"

"Hi, Miriam, this is actually Julieta," I say in a low voice.

"Ah, ma chérie, Julieta, how lovely to hear your voice," she says in a genuine tone. "I hope you received your gift?"

"Yes, thank you. It was very thoughtful of you."

"It was the least I could do for our hero. I'm still lobbying to get you a medal of sorts from the government, but I was told that at the very least, you'll get a thank-you letter. And, you know, you and I will have to come back to visit the Louvre again. I'll give you a private tour of the whole museum."

"Won't that take, like, days?" I ask.

She chuckles. "You're right, maybe not the whole museum."

I wonder if she'll still want to be my tour guide once she knows the truth. "Miriam?"

"Yes, Julieta?"

"I'm really sorry the diamond was taken from

India. If it ever leaves the Louvre, I hope it goes back to where it was found."

I guess I must have surprised her, because I only hear a sigh from her end.

"Thank you, Julieta," she says after a few seconds. "That's true. It was found in a mine in India and stolen from there. Hopefully one day it can go back to its true home through the correct channels."

"Do you think it will ever happen?" I ask, curious.

"I honestly don't know. I hope so. But it's not just the diamond. Thousands of pieces in museums around the world got there through theft or appropriation. But I would never dream of stealing the diamond back. Didn't you know it's cursed?"

48

After my exciting call with Miriam, the hours crawl by slowly, one after the other. Waiting for Mom and Dad to come back from the hospital is the equivalent of torture, in my opinion. They should have been back over half an hour ago. Robin, who's babysitting again, has tried to coax me into playing board games, a walk around the neighborhood, a movie, and eating.

I didn't want any of that.

Instead, I keep walking to the window and opening the shades, checking to see if Mom and Antonio are walking up the street, and then strutting back to my room, disappointed. Then, I repeat the process once more.

Finally, the lock clicks and the door opens.

"Hogar, dulce hogar," Mom says when she walks into the apartment.

I run and hug Mom carefully, since I don't want to hurt her. Dad walks in behind her carrying baby Antonio in the car seat. He looks tiny, swimming in the seat. His eyes are closed. He's wearing a little blue hat and a onesie that reads: I LOVE MY BIG SIS. I smile and swell up, proud to be his sister.

"And that's my cue to leave," Robin says.

Dad hands her a couple bills. "Thanks, Robin."

"Congratulations again," she says as she walks out the door.

Mom sits down in the rocking chair that Dad and I put together the night before. "So I hear you've been busy?"

"Yes!" I answer excitedly. "We're done with the crib, and obviously the chair you're sitting in." I count on two fingers. "We still have a couple of other items to put together, but Dad said those could wait, since Antonio won't be using them for a while."

Mom smiles. She looks exhausted, but so happy at the same time. "I see. But I was talking about the museum. I heard you got a call from Miriam?"

I put my hands behind my back and look sideways.

"Aw, it's nothing," I say, pretending I don't care. "I'm only getting an official thanks from the French government and an invitation to visit the Louvre anytime I want."

"Really?" Mom turns disbelievingly to Dad.

"Actually, yeah," he admits.

"I'm so proud, Julieta!" she exclaims.

I'm proud of myself too and can't hide it any longer, so I start jumping up and down waving my arms around.

"Shhh!" Mom and Dad say, both pointing at baby Antonio, who continues to sleep without a care in the world. I compromise and give tiny little jumps, swinging only my forearms. I must look pretty silly, because Mom and Dad start laughing.

I stop, suddenly remembering the gifts I brought back. "Oh, I almost forgot. I'll be right back."

I run back to my room and grab the box I wrapped last night in Christmas-themed wrapping paper—the only wrapping paper I could find around the house.

As I walk into the living room, I hold the gift behind my back. "Mom, we brought you something from our trip."

"You did?"

"Yes," I say. "Dad and I picked it out together."

"I'm sure I'll love it." She gives me a big smile.

Before handing over the box, I give it a little shake.

She opens the box and lifts out the snow globe. The Eiffel Tower stands inside the middle of the globe, surrounded by swirling snow.

"It's beautiful!" she says. "And guess what? *I* also have a surprise for you."

She takes out a folder from her overnight bag and hands it to me. I open it to find a single sheet of paper. It's a birth certificate. She turns to Dad and says, "It's for you too."

Dad sits on the armchair and motions me to his knee. "Let's see."

We both stare at the paper for a few seconds, trying to figure out what the surprise could be. Under *name* it reads: *Antonio H. Leal.*

I point at the *H* and look at Dad.

He shrugs and asks, "Erica, what does the *H* stand for?"

She smiles. "That's the surprise. It's up to the two of you to decide."

"Hypnos," I offer. "Since he's always sleeping."

"Horus," Dad counters.

"Heracles."

"Hapi."

"Hephaestus."

This is never going to end.

The True Story of the Regent Diamond

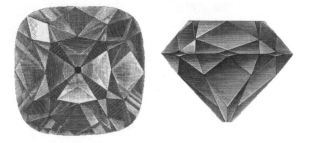

The Regent Diamond is also known as the Pitt Diamond, after Thomas Pitt, the man who brought it to Europe. It is one of the most valuable diamonds in the world and currently worth almost 74 million dollars. Just like in Julieta's story, the Regent has had quite an adventure throughout history.

The Regent was first discovered by an unnamed slave in 1698 in the Kollur Mine in India. The slave smuggled the diamond out of the mine by putting it in a large wound in his leg. Yuck! An English sea captain later stole it from the slave and sold it to Jamchand, an Indian merchant. Three years later, in 1701, Thomas Pitt, the president of Madras (an Indian city), bought it from Jamchand for 48,000 pagodas, a gold coined used by British, Dutch, and Indian people. The cost was roughly equal to 3,544,789 dollars today.

In 1704, Pitt decided to cut the diamond into pieces that could be worn. It took two years for a jeweler named Harris to finish the cushion cut, which is a square style with rounded corners. From the same stone, other smaller diamonds were produced and sold to Peter the Great of Russia. The biggest stone was eventually sold in 1717 to Philippe II, Duke of Orleans. At the time, Philippe was the French regent, which means he was in power until his nephew King Louis XV became old enough to rule. (Louis was seven years old at the time.) Since Philippe was the one who ordered the purchase of the diamond, the name "Regent" stuck, and it has been called that ever since.

Five years later in 1722, when Louis XV was twelve years old and old enough to become the ruler, the Regent Diamond was set into his coronation crown, but it didn't stay there for long. In 1775, it was moved into Louis XVI's coronation crown. However, Louis XVI's wife, Marie Antoinette, would also get a chance to wear it, because some years after his coronation, the Regent made its way into one of her hats.

Marie Antoinette didn't have her hat for long. In 1789, the French Revolution broke out. The French people were done being ruled by a royal class. Fighting broke out against the crown, and many people died. There was a lot of confusion, and the royal family was moved from Versailles to the Tuileries Palace inside Paris to keep the king and his family from fleeing. Louis XVI and Marie Antoinette were both executed. It was during this time that the Regent was stolen and hidden in an attic roof.

By the time Napoleon Bonaparte crowned himself emperor of France in 1804, the Regent had been rediscovered in that attic. Napoleon took the diamond into his possession and had it set into his sword belt and later his sword hilt.

After Napoleon's death, his widow, Archduchess Marie Louise of Austria, took the Regent back home with her to Austria around 1815. Her father, Francis II—also known as the Holy Roman Emperor— returned the diamond to France several years later. The French monarchy had it mounted onto three more crowns: one for Louis XVII, one for Charles X, and then another for Napoleon III.

And finally, in the mid-1800s, it was worn by a

woman once more. It was set into a diadem for Empress Eugenie, the wife of Napoleon III.

In 1887, the French crown jewels, worn by French kings and queens, were sold at an auction, but the Regent Diamond was saved and instead of being sold, was put on display at the Louvre, where it has stayed—except during World War II. During the war, it was taken to Chambord, France, and was hidden behind a stone panel to avoid it being stolen by the Nazis.

A lot of deadly things happened to those who have possessed or worn the Regent Diamond, and because of that, many believe it to be cursed. The slave who stole the diamond from the mine was killed by Thomas Pitt. Louis XVI and Marie Antoinette were decapitated. Louis XVIII and Napoleon III were both exiled. Charles X was forced to give up the throne and died of cholera.

So why did so many people want the diamond even

though it was believed to be cursed? Probably because it was and still is worth lots of money. The value of a diamond is determined by four things: color, clarity, weight, and cut. The color comes from the different gases present around the diamond when it was being formed. Clarity is when there are few imperfections inside the diamond. Its weight, or carat, determines its size. And finally, its cut, or shape, is what give a diamond its brilliance, symmetry, polish, and shine.

Before it was cut, the Regent Diamond was approximately 410 carats. That's huge! Now, after being cut, it measures 140.64 carats. Its amazing clarity and pale blue-and-white color make it quite distinct. All of these factors make the Regent Diamond one of the most valuable diamonds in the world with its 74-million-dollar price tag—the reason why many would ignore stories that the diamond is cursed.

To learn more about diamonds, visit gia.edu.

Why Julieta Thinks Athena Is Cool

Athena is the goddess of wisdom. Metis, her mother, was the goddess of prudence and Zeus's first wife. One day, Gaea (Mother Earth) warned Zeus that if Metis, who had become pregnant, bore him a son, he would grow up to take away Zeus's throne. Zeus became so afraid, he decided to avoid the problem altogether and swallowed Metis before her child was born, leaving her stuck in Zeus's head. Metis thought her child would need some protection before being born, so she hammered and hammered and created a helmet for her unborn child.

All the pounding gave Zeus a terrible headache, and he shrieked in pain. To help, Hephaestus (god of metalwork and fire) cracked Zeus's skull open with his tools. Athena stepped out, fully grown and wearing the helmet Metis created for her. And that's how Athena was born from Zeus's head.

Although Athena is mainly known as being the goddess of wisdom, she was also the goddess of courage, inspiration, law and justice, mathematics, strategic warfare, crafts, the arts, and skill. In times of peace, she inspired artists and helped warriors like Perseus in their quests. Nike, the goddess of victory, was her best friend.

The city of Athens is named after Athena as well. She is often depicted with an owl, a symbol of wisdom, on her shoulder.

The Art Within the Story

GROUP OF THE THREE GRACES

The statue of the *Group of the Three Graces* that Julieta and her family take a picture with is a stone sculpture from the second century C.E. The Graces, or the Greek minor goddesses of beauty, were believed to be daughters of Zeus and Eurynome. They are named Aglaea (splendor), Euphrosyne (mirth), and Thalia (good cheer and festivity). The Graces welcomed ashore Aphrodite, the goddess of beauty, as she rose from the sea, and they became her handmaids. In different parts of Greece, there are different numbers of Graces. How-

ever, they all promote joy and the pleasures of life. The statue of the Graces stands about four feet tall and can be found in the New York Metropolitan Museum of Art under the accession number 2010.260.

ATHENA PARTHENOS

The armless *Athena Parthenos (the Virgin Goddess)* statue in the MFA which Julieta sets off to see at the begin-

ning of the book is five feet tall and made of stone. The goddess wears a helmet that features a Pegasus on each side with a sphinx, but only the paws of the sphinx remain. Other images carved into the sculpture are deer, griffins, and snakes. The accession number is 1980.196.

ATHENA PROMACHOS

The MFA's bronze statuette that everyone thinks Julieta borrowed but Dr. Jenkins had only moved from its exhibit is the *Athena Promachos*. It dates back to 510 to 500 B.C.E. and was first discovered in Minorca, Greece. It is less than five inches tall, and is missing a spear, helmet, and shield. Its accession number is 54.145.

BUST REPLICA OF ZEUS

The bust replica of Zeus in which Jacques smuggles the diamond is based on this statue from the Louvre's collection called *Jupiter of Smyrna* (c. 250 B.C.E.). It was brought to Versailles for Louis XIV in 1680. The statue uses the name *Jupiter* because when the Romans conquered Greece in 146 B.C.E., the Romans kept the Greek religion and their gods and simply changed the names.

LA VICTOIRE DE SAMOTHRACE

The grand marble statue at the Louvre that Julieta's father surprises her with is *La Victoire de Samothrace*. It was discovered on the island of Rhodes in Greece and measures 2.75 meters, or a little over 9 feet, tall. Its base is almost as tall as the statue itself, so of course Julieta needed some help to pose with it.

The winged goddess is believed to be depicted as standing on the prow of a ship, and it once stood overlooking the Sanctuary of the Great Gods on the island of Samothrace in the northwest Aegean Sea.

Glossary

ALI BABA'S CAVE: Ali Baba's cave is from the Middle Eastern folk story "Ali Baba and the Forty Thieves," found in Antoine Galland's translation of the Arabic collection *One Thousand and One Nights*. The cave is filled with uncountable riches and can only be entered by saying "Open Sesame."

ALIBI: Evidence that someone was at a location other than the crime scene, proving they could not have committed the crime.

ARC DE TRIOMPHE: Considered the biggest arch in the world, the Arc de Triomphe overlooks the Champs-Élysées. The arch was commissioned by Napoleon Bonaparte in 1806. Visitors can climb the arch and look out from the top.

ART HANDLER: Art handlers usually work in museums and art galleries preparing art pieces and historical objects for show and transportation. They make sure everything is handled carefully while packing, unpacking, moving, installing, and bringing down the art for exhibitions.

ASTERIX AND OBELIX: Asterix and Obelix are best friends and the protagonists in René Goscinnys and Albert Uderzo's comic titled *Asterix and Obelix*. Easily recognizable by their mustaches and their depiction as Gauls, Asterix and Obelix go on silly adventures throughout the ancient world.

BENEDICTINE NUNS: The Benedictine Nuns are one of the oldest orders of nuns in the Catholic Church. They dedicate their lives to the service of God and focus their activities on prayer and adoration.

"BUENOS DÍAS SEÑOR SOL" BY JUAN GABRIEL: "Buenos Días Señor Sol," the song Julieta sings to the newborn Antonio, is about self-improvement, gratefulness, and love. The song was written by Juan Gabriel, the famed Mexican singer, songwriter, and actor who wrote over 1,800 songs.

CHILAQUILES: Chilaquiles are a traditional Mexican dish made by cutting and frying tortillas. These tortilla chips are bathed in red or green chile sauce, and cheese is often added on top. Chilaquiles sometimes include other ingredients such as chicken, beef, eggs, or chorizo.

EIFFEL TOWER: The Eiffel Tower is one of the most famous structures in the world, designed by Gustave Eiffel and erected in 1889. Measuring 324 meters (about 1,063 feet) high, it was the tallest building in the world until the Chrysler Building was built in New York in 1933.

ELOTES: Also called *esquites*, elotes are often referred to as Mexican street corn. Elotes are made of boiled or grilled ears of corn with multiple toppings. The most popular toppings include mayo, chile powder, lime juice, and cheese.

ESCARGOTS: Having nothing to do with goats, *escargot* means "snail" in French. Escargots are considered a delicacy in France to eat and can often be found on restaurant menus.

FLEUR-DE-LIS: A fleur-de-lis is a stylized lily with three petals that meet at the bottom. The design was previously used in the coats of arms of French kings.

GALERIE DES GLACES—HALL OF MIRRORS: The Hall of Mirrors (1689) is the most famous room at the Palace of Versailles. It first served as a room for people waiting to meet the king as well as a place to hold weddings and balls. In 1919, it was used for the signing of the Treaty of Versailles, which signaled the end of World War I.

HINDUISM: One of the oldest religions in the world, Hinduism developed around 500 B.C.E. in India, and is popular in South Asia. A polytheistic religion made of many smaller traditions, Hinduism proposes the possibility of reincarnation, or multiple lives.

INTERPOL: Officially named the International Criminal Police Organization, INTERPOL has members from 194 countries. It serves as a data access point on crimes and criminals for the police in the member countries to "work together and make the world a safer place."

JEAN D'ARC—JOAN OF ARC: Joan of Arc was a young French heroine who, in the fifteenth century, led France in battle against the English. At twelve, Joan began to hear voices and have visions which she interpreted as signs from God asking her to lead the French troops. Joan went on to recapture Orléans and Troyes, which had been taken by the English during the Hundred Years' War. At the age of nineteen, she was burned at the stake for witchcraft and heresy.

METROPOLITAN MUSEUM OF ART: The Metropolitan Museum of Art, also known as the Met, is located in New York City. Considered one of the largest museums in the world, the Met is home to more than two million historical and artistic pieces.

MUSÉE DU LOUVRE—THE LOUVRE MUSEUM: Located in Paris, France, The Louvre is the most-visited art museum in the world. Its impressive collection includes objects from all over the globe, dating from prehistoric civilizations to the mid-1800s. Some of the world's most famous pieces of art are housed there, like Leonardo da Vinci's painting, *Mona Lisa* (c. 1503–1506) and the Greek statue *Venus de Milo* (101 B.C.E.). Its structure was originally built in 1546 to serve as the royal residence before it became a museum in 1793. In 1989, its famous glass pyramid entrance, designed by I. M. Pei, a Chinese American architect, was added. Like many other museums, some of the Louvre's collections and art pieces were unfortunately acquired without permission from other countries.

MUSEUM OF FINE ARTS, BOSTON: The Museum of Fine Arts, or MFA, in Boston, Massachusetts is the fifth-largest art museum in the US. It held 5,600 pieces of art when it opened in 1870, but has grown to almost 500,000 pieces as of the printing of this book.

NAVE: A nave is the central part of a church, usually a long rectangular space, where most of the people will sit, stand, or kneel when attending services. Usually, the altar or centerpiece of the church is located at the end of the nave.

NAZIS: The Nazis, led by Adolph Hitler, were a German political party responsible for the outbreak of World War II in 1939. Known for their brutal racism, anti-Semitism, and the genocide of millions, they also stole hundreds of thousands of art pieces during the war. To this date, thousands of art pieces are still missing or have not been returned to their rightful owners.

NIKE: Nike, the Greek goddess of speed, strength, and victory, is often displayed as Athena's companion. Her parents were the Titan Pallas and the goddess Styx, who, in Greek mythology, is a river separating Earth from the Underworld. Nike often carried a wreath to crown the victors in battles or games. This is why Olympian athletes, even today, are crowned with wreaths.

NOTRE-DAME DE PARIS: The Notre-Dame de Paris (Our Lady of Paris) is a medieval Catholic cathedral in Paris, France. Built from 1160 to 1260, it is known for its flying buttresses and rose windows. In 2019, its roof caught fire, risking many of the historical artifacts it housed, including the Crown of Thorns, said to have been placed on the head of Jesus during his crucifixion. After the fire, the artifacts were taken to the Louvre for safekeeping while the cathedral is being rebuilt.

PAIN AU CHOCOLAT: Meaning "chocolate bread," pain au chocolat is a French pastry made by layering thin sheets of yeast-leavened dough with butter—which makes them puffy and flaky when baked. It is then filled with chocolate and folded into a rectangular shape.

PERPETUAL ADORATION OF THE BLESSED SACRAMENT: For Catholics, Jesus Christ is believed to be wholly present in the *Blessed Sacrament* (also called the *Eucharist*), which consists of the sacred bread, called the *Host*, and the sacred wine. The adoration of the Blessed Sacrament usually takes the form of meditation, prayer, and song, which in some Catholic parishes is available all day and all night for people to visit. This is called *perpetual adoration*. There is a constant rotation of people, so that a person is praying, or guarding, the exposed Blessed Sacrament day and night.

SACRÉ-CŒUR BASILICA: The Sacré-Cœur Basilica (built from 1875 to 1914) sits atop Montmartre, a tall hill within Paris's eighteenth arrondissement. It's known for its large staircase of ninety steps that visitors can take to reach it, as well as its domed roof above the altar showing *Christ in Glory*, designed by Olivier Merson. The chapels within and around the Sacré-Cœur Basilica are dedicated to different saints and orders.

SARI: A sari is a traditional dress worn by women in South Asia that is made of a length of fabric, usually colorful cotton or silk. The fabric is worn draped around the body.

SPIROGRAPH: Spirographs are drawing tools with gearlike shapes, such as rectangles, circles, and triangles, that spin around another shape to create intricate designs. Spirographs first became popular in the 1960s.

TINTIN: The *Tintin* comics, created by Georges Remi under his pen name Hergé, take their name from their protagonist Tintin, a reporter and adventurer who travels around the world with his pet dog Snowy. The comics are set in the twentieth century.

VERSAILLES: King Louis XIII of France began building Versailles as a small hunting lodge in 1623—but it wasn't quite big enough for him, so he made it bigger in 1634. His son, Louis XIV, expanded it even more in 1682 and made it the main residence for the French court. Later, Louis XVI renovated the interior and built a smaller palace for his wife, Marie Antoinette. In 1837, fifty years after the royal family was forced to leave for the Tuileries Palace in Paris, Versailles opened as a museum. Today, it is also known for its beautiful sculptured gardens and Hall of Mirrors.

ZEUS: Zeus, king of the Greek gods, was a fighter from a young age. With his mother, Rhea, and his brothers and sisters, he was able to dethrone his father, the Titan Cronus, who had been swallowing his children, afraid one of them would rise up against him. After defeating Cronus, Zeus was then crowned Lord of the Universe and shared his power with his brothers and sisters. He is often depicted with lightning bolts and has many children, both gods and demigods. Athena, the goddess of wisdom, is believed to be his favorite.

Author's Note and Acknowledgments

I wish I could say I had the perfect plan for this book from its original conception, but that would be a lie. First came Julieta's character, springing about, always thirsty for adventure. Then came all the bumbling and tumbling on my part to give her a story. That story changed a lot as it grew and matured, but Julieta's enthusiastic love for mythology and art always remained. It was always my hope to show her respect for those who inspire and create art.

Throughout my research, I became more and more aware of the thousands of art pieces that were stolen, stripped, and pillaged from their original creators, homes, and countries throughout the ages. I wanted to bring awareness to this issue, not to condemn or alienate, but to hopefully inspire understanding, admiration, and reverence to the history of each art piece we are lucky to encounter in our lives.

I would like to thank those instrumental in helping me bring Julieta and her adventures to life: Lee & Low Books and Tu Books. Stacy Whitman, my amazing publisher, for being there with me from the beginning and your faith in this project! To my editor, Elise McMullen-Ciotti, and the wonderful copyeditor Shveta Thakrar and book designer Sammy Yuen. Thanks also to artist Olivia Aserr and for your beautiful interpretation of Julieta on the cover.

To all my Simmons people, professors, and peers for your support, especially Cathie Mercier: Thank you for encouraging me to submit my story to Tu Books' New Visions Award.

Mom, thank you for inspiring my love for Greek mythology. And Tito Raúl, who always made sure I had a book in my hand.

Finally, thank you to my three graces: Grace McKinney, for being my buddy in the trenches, your honest opinions, and dealing with my freak-outs; Graciela Quintero Pasaret for letting me ask so many questions about diamonds and answering them all; and the grace of God, without which I am nothing.

About the Author

LUISANA DUARTE ARMENDÁRIZ grew up on the Juárez, Mexico–El Paso, Texas border. After living in Rhode Island, Boston, and Manila, Philippines, she now works as a Dean of Discipline at a boarding school in Michigan. A writer and graphic designer, Luisana earned her BA from the University of Texas at El Paso (go, Miners!), and her MA/MFA in Children's Literature and Writing for Children from Simmons University in Boston. She won the 2018 Lee & Low/Tu Books New Visions Award for her debut novel, *Julieta and the Diamond Enigma*. Like Julieta, Luisana never tires of learning new things. Unlike Julieta, she has never jumped into a fountain . . . yet.

Photo Credits

Photo of the marble statue of the *Group of the Three Graces*, residing at The Metropolitan Museum of Art, Heilbrunn Timeline of Art History, licensed under public domain via The Metropolitan Museum of Art and Creative Commons.

Photo of the statue *Athena Parthenos* (the Virgin Goddess) © 2020, Museum of Fine Arts, Boston. Used with permission.

Photo of the statue *Athena Promachos* © 2020, Museum of Fine Arts, Boston. Used with permission.

Photo of *The Winged Victory of Samothrace* statue after its 2014 restoration, residing at the Department of Greek, Etruscan, and Roman Antiquities in the Musée du Louvre, by "Rijin S," source licensed under (CC-BY-SA 4.0) via Wikimedia Commons, 2015.

Photo of the marble statue *Jupiter of Smyrna* residing at the Department of Greek, Etruscan, and Roman Antiquities in the Musée de Louvre, by Marie-Lan Nguyen and licensed under public domain via Wikimedia Commons, 2009.

Photo of "Regent (diamond) black" by Ahnode, licensed under public domain via Wikimedia Commons, 2009.

Photo of Thomas Pitt painting by English portrait painter Godfrey Kneller, by "Rudolf 1922," licensed under public domain via Wikimedia Commons, 2005.

Photo of Empress Eugenie, 1856, by French photographer Jean Baptiste Gustave Le Gray, licensed under public domain via Wikimedia Commons, 2011.

Art of Goddess Athena, by "Mark22," free download, goodfon.com.